Praise for *Dear Cyborgs*

BOMB Magazine, "Best of 2017," selected by Chris Kraus
Vol. 1 Brooklyn, "Favorite Fiction Books of 2017"
Chicago Review of Books, "Best Books of 2017"
The Millions, "Most Anticipated"
Literary Hub, "Favorite Books of 2017"
Wired, "Essential Summer Reads"
Buzzfeed, "Exciting New Books You Need to Read This Summer"

"Transfixing from page to page, filled with digressive meditations on small talk and social protest, superheroes, terrorism, the art world, and the status of being marginal. . . . There's an intoxicating, whimsical energy on every page. Everything from radical art to political protest gets absorbed into the rhythms of everyday life."   **—Hua Hsu, *The New Yorker***

"A novel about art and resistance, and how they may spur each other on, or frustrate their respective goals. In structure it resembles the great mid-century metafictions. . . . Eugene Lim's super-comrades, with their cultural disaffection and nuanced political opinions, offer a rather more compelling version of a collective consciousness."
                     —David Hobbs, *Times Literary Supplement*

"Two radically different story lines are cleverly tied together in this short, sly, unorthodox novel. . . . The core relationships, whether they're between estranged childhood friends or opinionated superhumans, are real and profoundly moving."   **—*Publishers Weekly*, starred review**

"A novel of ideas, small, elegant ideas about art and protest, and one of the most striking literary works to emerge from the Occupy movement. . . . I had expected the decade's wave of protests to yield a raft of conventional social novels—some earnest, some satirical, perhaps not a few reactionary—but in *Dear Cyborgs* Lim has delivered something far more idiosyncratic, intricate, and useful: a novel that resists and subverts conventions at every turn."
                    —Christian Lorentzen, *New York Magazine*

"Blew me away with its deceptively blithe mixture of cryptic humor, philosophical ingenuity, and genuine political yearning. It made me think of Robert Bolaño and Tom McCarthy. I'm hoping to reread it soon for inspiration."   **—Jonathan Lethem, *Chicago Review of Books***

"I know I'm reading a good book when it makes me mutter, What *is* this? Eugene Lim's slim and very weird *Dear Cyborgs* evoked that response in me plenty of times.... *Dear Cyborgs* is like the image inside a kaleidoscope, especially if that image comes from the midnineties cyberpunk-tinged dream of a middle-aged vegan asleep in Zuccotti Park circa 2011. In other words: it certainly keeps you on your toes."

—**Jeffery Gleaves,** *The Paris Review*

"Haunting. . . . Should vault [Lim] into the first rank of American writers." —**Ross Barkan,** *The Village Voice*

"Surreal, unpredictable, and filled with protest. Lim packs an impressive range of topics into one slim and absorbing novel; everything from comic books to the avant garde to revolution gets its due. This constantly shifting ground seems to transmit a warily hopeful message: any number of possible futures are within our grasp—if not better, then at least different." —**Jess Bergman, Literary Hub**

"A smart, inventive, highly unconventional novel that explores themes of resistance, art, capitalism, and contemporary culture."

—**Jarry Lee, BuzzFeed**

"A mind-bending, form-shifting book about superheroes, protest, the art world, Asian American friendship, and the abyss. What's most striking is how brilliantly (and seamlessly) Lim employs slippery narrative techniques in this novel in stories within conversations within dreams."

—**James Yeh,** *VICE*

"The most lucid book I've read lately. . . . It is rare to encounter self-aware, genre-spliced postmodernism that is this worldly and purposeful, or pop that is this utilitarian, serious, and searching, or timely state-of-the-nation reckonings that are this optimistic, open, and kindhearted. . . . Quite an achievement."

—**J. W. McCormack, Electric Literature**

"Relevant, important fiction in the time of political chaos. Superheroes and artistic characters fill the pages with musings and arguments about what matters and what's vital in a life riddled with uncertainties."

—**Sara Cutaia,** *Chicago Review of Books*

SEARCH HISTORY

CONCERNING THE

*Adventures,
Quests, and Setbacks of*

FRANK EXIT,
HIS FRIENDS
&
OTHER STRANGERS

OF FAR FLUNG AND NEARBY ORIGIN

Caught in the Winds of

la huida hacia adelante

OR

The Unfolding

OR

The Flux

Oracle (1967–1968) by Miyoko Ito

SEARCH HISTORY

Eugene Lim

COFFEE HOUSE PRESS

Minneapolis

2021

Image credits: *Ning Mountain* © Shannon Steneck; *Emergence of Locomotion Behaviors* image courtesy of DeepMind; *Oracle* courtesy of Karen Lennox Gallery; Pat Morita image courtesy of Herald Examiner Collection/Los Angeles Public Library.

Coffee House Press books are available to the trade through our primary distributor, Consortium Book Sales & Distribution, cbsd.com or (800) 283-3572. For personal orders, catalogs, or other information, write to info@coffeehousepress.org.

Coffee House Press is a nonprofit literary publishing house. Support from private foundations, corporate giving programs, government programs, and generous individuals helps make the publication of our books possible. We gratefully acknowledge their support in detail in the back of this book.

LIBRARY OF CONGRESS CATALOGING-IN-PUBLICATION DATA

Names: Lim, Eugene, author.
Title: Search history / Eugene Lim.
Description: Minneapolis : Coffee House Press, 2021.
Identifiers: LCCN 2021020999 (print) | LCCN 2021021000 (ebook) |
    ISBN 9781566896177 (trade paperback) | ISBN 9781566896269 (epub)
Subjects: GSAFD: Satire. | LCGFT: Psychological fiction.
Classification: LCC PS3612.I46 S43 2021 (print) | LCC PS3612.I46
    (ebook) | DDC 813/.6—dc23
LC record available at https://lccn.loc.gov/2021020999
LC ebook record available at https://lccn.loc.gov/2021021000

PRINTED IN THE UNITED STATES OF AMERICA
28 27 26 25 24 23 22 21   1 2 3 4 5 6 7 8

In memory of Ning Li, 1974–2017

But he warned me that in this case I should not expect subtle tricks, for this was a Hollywood movie, and not even, any longer, the Hollywood of John Ford or Hitchcock but rather an industry deeply infiltrated by a young audience brought up on comic books and phantasmagorias, an audience with its taste buds savaged by extraterrestrials and superheroes. So, a break from realism was the least one could expect. After all, they had every right to take that break: they were the ones making the movie and they could do whatever they felt like. And, one had to admit that if one was not very demanding, this unexpected introduction of an element of fantasy was worthwhile, if only for the suggestive symmetries it conjured up.

—CÉSAR AIRA, CONVERSATIONS

Does a dog have Buddha-nature?

—THE GATELESS GATE (無門關)

To me, a book is the closest thing there is to a human being.

—FRAN LEBOWITZ

THE PROLOGUE TO THE PROLOGUE

or

A WARNING TO THE READER

or

THE ADVENTURE OF THE READER

or

THE OLD WINDUP

THE LIBRARY OF BABEL = INTERNET

The thing about the infinite library is that step one is to know the book you want and step two is figuring out how to get to its location.

The final book is : a murder mystery, an outdated owner's manual, a poetry chapbook, a shy crank's monograph, pornography, a broken novel. If you read it, then : unicorns and rainbows, tumor shrinkage and the dead restored, moonbeams and polka dots, orgasms and money.

To find this book of answers you begin reading other books, which teases enlightenment but more often leads to chaos, intoxication, pointless idle, blood oath, masturbation, fiancées, and dance.

This is the adventure of the reader.

Prologue

Half my heart is crushed, and the other half is on fire.
—BHAIRAVI DESAI

It was no longer possible to understand being poor or defeated. Which meant she could no longer imagine it. This worried her because if she ever *were* to become defeated or poor, she would then feel like a fool—and this might somehow be more painful than the destitution. More importantly, this realization worried her because it meant she no longer felt human.

The dysthymic artificial intelligence scientist took a book of poetry off the shelf and sat on her couch.

What was she ushering in and what was a grand program for which she was simply helpless agent? Senseless to think about, she thought, as she sipped her diet beer with ice.

She had purposefully cultivated a taste for this drink after reading that a billionaire, who could obviously consume whatever he desired, had made it his beverage of choice. Typical of her sense of humor was the irony of the blandly effervescent flavor but also the discipline to carry out the conceptual joke to its regular daily end.

She was not on the team employed by the galactic corporation that had created a machine that had taught itself to play an ancient, spatial, seemingly impossibly open game well enough to repeatedly and decisively defeat the world's human champions.

She was merely an associate professor in a community college, but such were the economic interest and forecasting that even her low-rung campus needed to offer courses in the field.

Twenty-five years ago, she had wanted to be a poet. Her parents had told her to be sensible, and so she'd majored in computer science at Stanford. Her classmates had gone on to form the titanic corporations that had transformed—and continue to transform—everyone's lives, while she had listlessly spun slowly down the academic helix, plagued by both suicidal ideation and alcoholism. Her parents were now dead, and she was teaching spastic undergrads at St. Francis College of Southern New Jersey.

That's the end of that story. These paragraphs were written by a robot named César Aira.

The robot named César Aira was going through a relatively amicable divorce with his wife, a famous documentary filmmaker and part-time reiki healer named Onoto Watanna. One of Onoto's clients was a gallery owner, and this gallerist had invited Onoto to an opening.

César was still living with Onoto and their two kids but now slept on the couch. It was amicable enough a divorce that they would still go out together, and Onoto invited César to the opening. The art was atrocious and consisted of white people in yellowface reading from the text of the Chinese Exclusion Act and transcriptions of ICE raid recordings. Autotune was used to have these voices sing to the melody of "This Land Is Your Land." The art was said to be by a secret collective named "McArthur Grant," but everyone knew it was the product of a famous older white artist. He was at the center of the party with his new, younger Chinese American girlfriend.

Proof that the art indeed was terrible, at least to Onoto, became evident by how much everyone at the party professed the opposite. Onoto was introduced briefly to the artist, a man of leathered complexion and gleaming white hair. He had what might have been called *rugged* good looks, and Onoto found him both easy to look at and reptilian. Much later she would become friends with his then girlfriend, a woman who had since broken up with him and had admitted the dalliance was pure opportunism on her part to see if she could become famous by association. It had only partly worked because she had caused a gossipy stir when, in an interview, she claimed that the yellowface performance had been her idea to see how racist a piece the art world would accept. She said the idea had been fascinatingly easy to plant in the older artist's mind as one of his own. Of course, the older artist denied this as well as the racism; instead he claimed it was a transgressive gesture misunderstood by the self-elected tone police. Onoto was skeptical about the woman's motivations, but she enjoyed her boldness.

Meanwhile, back at the party,

Meanwhile, back at the party, César the robot is going outside to have a cigarette. He finds himself standing next to a morose-looking man who has just walked outside to do the same. The man introduces himself as Kenny Golddigger, and César, in an uncharacteristic moment of dissembling, says his own name is Vanity Place. The two discuss the show, which both hated and thought preposterous, in the most glowing terms.

Kenny then says to the robot named César who had introduced himself as Vanity, "I'm outraged."

Vanity takes a puff of his cigarette and says, "Oh yeah?"

Kenny says, "I've just found out that the daughter of a billionaire oil industrialist has started a press to publish poetry. The billionaire oil industrialist has financed wars, white supremacists, and climate change denial. The daughter is using writers of color and excellent poetry to whitewash blood money."

"Better than equestrian sports," Vanity says.

"It's an abomination," says Kenny.

"Cash rules everything around me."

"It's disgusting."

"Laughlin's fortune came from a union-busting steel company."

"What?"

"It's the Wu coming through."

"What?"

"I've a solution."

"Yeah? What."

"Write an open letter saying that in order to move the publishing enterprise's function from whitewashing blood money closer to reparations, the press should exclusively publish climate-crisis fiction by indigenous writers."

Kenny Golddigger laughs at this, stubs out his cigarette, and then walks back inside the party. He seems to dismiss Vanity's suggestion. However, the idea so grows in his mind that the following week he posts the proposal on his personal website. It generates a huge spike in traffic. A month after this, Kenny is murdered in what appears to be an unrelated car accident.

"All is," Vanity says, "vanity."

The robot named César mutters this phrase out loud upon returning to the party.

"No shit, Sherlock," says Onoto, joining him at the crowd's periphery.

And then, instead of being at an elite gallery opening in Chelsea, the fiction transforms them into two young women working under a fume hood, soldering bits under bright lights at a cell phone factory in Dongguan, China.

"I just found out that the owner's daughter moved," says the factory worker who, despite changing location and gender, is still named César (though perhaps no longer a robot—but who could tell?), "to Vancouver, Canada."

"How did you find out?" asks the other factory worker who, despite changing location and occupation, is still named Onoto, and adds, "It's just a fad. All the Chinese millionaire heirs are doing it."

César says that she'd read about it while scrolling through the unending communally written epic poem that everyone de facto agreed was the best piece of literature humanity had ever created. It contained multitudes. "I read about it on Weibo," she says.

César and Onoto then go suddenly quiet as a supervisor screams, "No talking!"

After the supervisor walks past, they resume their conversation in careful whispers and with strategic turning to avoid their moving mouths being spotted by the surveillance cameras. Onoto asks, "By the way, how's your poetry going? Your last book did really well. Many many people hated it as opposed to being entirely oblivious of it or indifferent to it."

"Thanks, yes, it did really well."

"And now?"

"You know, it's funny. At my last job when I was standing on an assembly line putting thousands and thousands of tiny rubber caps into place on wireless routers for hours at a time, I was oddly happy, composing my poems in my head, songs about the river crabs that used to frolic near my parents' home, or a ditty about how my heart had been broken last winter, or a surreal poem written from the point of view of Xi Jinping's bedroom slippers squashing a rice bunny while multiplying eight by eight, and it all felt unconfined and liberated, actually, despite the hours of repetitive labor. But."

"Yes?"

"But something changed. I think it was when [Douglas Schifter] killed himself in the factory dormitory."

"He was such a sad sack."

"No! He was just like us. I used to meet him in the cantina and play cards with him, and he would ask me to recite my poems to him. He was funny and always knew where the best, cheap lunch spots were."

"Anyway, what does this have to do with your poetry?"

"I don't know. Now, when I'm soldering these circuit boards into place, standing for hours at a time as they come down the assembly line, well, I've begun to feel exhausted and sad. And I no longer compose poetry but think only of the Foxconn suicides and how people have to act like machines in order not to starve, only to eventually be replaced by actual machines, and how eventually everyone will die and become like whatever [Douglas Schifter] became—and what's even the point!"

"Hey now! Hey there. Hey. You can't do that. Don't do that to yourself. Don't give in to the gloom. You know what I think about while I'm snapping these plastic backings onto wearable fitness monitors all day long? I think about the interconnectedness of all things and how strangely destruction can lead to creation and vice versa."

"What do you mean?"

Before Onoto could react, a supervisor rushed over to scream at them again, so instead of listening to such invective, the fiction again transformed the duo into a plastic bag and the nubbin remaining from a little-used toddler teething ring, which floated among similar detritus in a wide spiral of trash drifting in the Atlantic.

The jetsam named Onoto responded to the flotsam named César, "Remember when we went to that art opening several paragraphs and reincarnations ago?"

"Yes."

"And there were those actors in yellowface singing in autotune?"

"Yes."

"What did you think of that?"

"I thought it contrived but better than the cheap, facile symbols we've now become."

"Not the reincarnation. What do you think of autotune?"

"Oh. Um, I guess I think of it as ugly, debased music to be consumed by the anesthetized. What's more an incredibly contagious musical virus that was born from a petrochemical engineer trying to use sound to extract more oil from the ground."

"Well, I take the opposite view."

"Which is."

"It's the new Moog. The idiom for the next evolutionary stage. A new aesthetic: music *by* cyborgs *for* cyborgs. And even if it ends in tears or flood or fire, even then it'll all continue somehow, even if it's just indestructible polymers eroding in a whirlpool of pollution or smoldering embers cooling after a nuclear fire but before furry lichens begin the process of greenery rising back. I have enduring faith in one thing: that the flux is necessary, absolute, and will never end."

"I have no need of such bullshit," types César, slumping into the chair at her cubicle desk, now reincarnated as one of a battalion of low-level censors at a social media corporation that has yet to develop an algorithm for reliably identifying pornographic content. She is online and chatting with her friend Onoto, who is now a scab teacher employed across the country to break a strike at a rural middle school and currently proctoring a multiple-choice three-hour-long exam and thus (like her students) bored, and so trolling César for entertainment, who adds, "And you know what else? This entire opening of recycled symbols of crisis is just a metonym of my daily experience with the internet. Thank god at least we haven't yet spoken of the upcoming elections."

"Please don't. Let's not—" texts Onoto to César as they both

wink completely out of existence so are unable to hear the words echoing in the reader's mind, a phrase that she was about to complete, and which has become metaphor for everyone's habit, one of gleefully losing hours to self-hypnosis. That is, Onoto's sudden but timely disappearance occurs before she can type: *go down that rabbit hole.*

"Come on! I've an idea."

No Machine Could Do It

I was surprised at the work because it was a well-structured novel. But there are still some problems [to overcome] to win the prize, such as character descriptions.

—SATOSHI HASE

THE DYSTHYMIC ARTIFICIAL INTELLIGENCE SCIENTIST WHO WISHED she'd become a poet extracts herself from the story written by the robot named César Aira by putting down her glass of now diluted diet beer and rising from the couch. All goes dark except for a spotlight shining on a hastily constructed pinewood stage. One hears footsteps clacking. She finds her mark, blinking a few times in the harsh light. She says:

Grief has changed me. Various deaths, the death of my best friend, the death of my parents, "littler" deaths pinging like raindrops around me, other more booming larger and closer deaths—and each a spiritual tremor, some annihilating earthquakes. And only now after digesting them, partially or whole, it seems I might finally begin to acknowledge all the loss that seemed inevitably to come with life. Prior to the deaths of my parents, before I was forever orphaned, in that era of their slow and then sudden decline, the saying that most made sense to me, that most articulated the changeover, was something I had heard years prior. A stranger had said it to me at a bar. Someone had quoted to me an old Yiddish saying: *When the father gives to the child, both laugh. And when the child gives to the father, both cry.* At the time I remember thinking, *What about the* mother? *When does* she *laugh and cry?* But subtracting the chauvinism, it's still an accurate description of a certain tide turning. How much delight my daughter used to get from a toy, something cheap and foolish to purchase for her—like a plastic bauble in a bubble from the coin-operated machine in front of the supermarket. *Please, Mommy. Pleeeeease, can I have one?* Why should I succumb to her importunings for such a stupid and, in fact, detrimental gift—one that inculcates within her not only a toxic materialism, but, like a gambler's fallacy, incentivizes a future habit of similar whiny requests? Because she calls me her *angel* when I give her the coins to operate the machine, because she giggles at the clear plastic bubble holding inside it—oh real joy—a plastic pullback motorcycle in the shape of a bumblebee. *Look at,* she tells strangers, *what mommy got me!* So the corruption is tied intrinsically with those first joys. Right from the beginning, purity impossible. Which isn't the problem: purity. No, that's no longer it, though for some time I admit it drove me. That was the wannabe poet within me, some teenager caught in arrested development, crusading, hardcore, a vision unmuddied by experience. Whom, by the way, I don't disparage. That's the spirit that will save us if anything will save us. But now. Now, it's no longer the vexing question, the day-to-day problem. *Now,* it's just a question of the loss. The losing and the loss. Now it's trying not to die so much every day, to not have the dying happen around me so much, to not see the dying even in that which is coming to life, to not be crushed every moment by the loss the loss the loss. In the city you run into someone at the movies or at a poetry reading or, less often, in line at the DMV, and you think, *Hey, there's my friend!* But the sweet, tenuous link between people that we name so easily as friendship can barely be held in the mind. I like to go to lunch one-on-one with a friend. That's what this is all about, what we're leading up to. That kind of lunch. That kind of lunch is the best. A casual meal and maybe you'll do something together after, maybe you'll spend the whole day and night together, or maybe it'll be just an hour or so and then you're both off. In the middle of life I found myself at various times in darkish diners and overheated or undercooled dives and compared notes on relative states of entropy and dissolution with a dozen or so Virgils who ate overdressed Cobb salads, icy mul-naengmyeons, fluffy sandwiches de miga, meaty momos, or hockey-puck cheeseburger deluxes, and we looked across battered and crumbled tables at each other, trying to name the things we could name—particularly the pretty nimbused phantoms we were in the middle of losing, but also the movie stars in something we saw last week as well as the gossip about the wrong turns of others. Hidden in the jibes and tales and joshing, of course, were those things we couldn't quite name but which we might make a gesture or joke toward, and also we'd laugh at, or call out, each other's sentimentality and romanticism, and maybe most importantly we would leave unsaid the things we couldn't bear or care or, for whatever reason, were unable to even think about. Like, for instance, several years ago I met for lunch my friend Jean, who used to go by Gene. Jean had transitioned after I first met her so sometimes I still misgendered her as Gene, which wasn't so offensive *to her*, so she claimed, but still it was embarrassing for me when I'd catch myself doing it. Old habits being tough to break. "How's it hanging, Gene?" I'd say, and she would smile brightly, as would I, because, in fact, occasions for us to get together were far too rare (though neither of us knew why). We were meeting for lunch near my apartment in Jackson Heights. It was a warm enough spring afternoon that we'd grabbed some empanadas from a Uruguayan bakery, made a second trip for some Vietnamese ice coffees, and taken our paper bags and plastic cups to sit on a park bench in the sun on a little grass-and-dirt half-block that passed for a park in our city. In other words, a perfect lunch. Jean said:

I'D BECOME FRIENDS WITH A PUBLIC INTELLECTUAL.

He handled everything: scandal, sex, politics, political sex scandals, racism, weather, the racism of weather, Japanese cartoons. Everything was under his purview, but his specialty was: The Future. He was a much more successful colleague at the university where I would occasionally adjunct. Several years ago, entirely by accident, when collecting some papers from our department's office, not knowing who he was, I saw him standing next to the faculty mailboxes with a copy of a book I'd just read. I was younger and new to the place and excitable—and so I started up a brief conversation about the book.

I think because I wasn't awestruck, because I'd no idea who he was, the conversation went smoothly. And a few days afterward we continued the conversation, which was rather pleasant, and soon after, we more or less became friends.

We had some important interests in common, but these were not quite overlapping enough that there was any real sense of competition between us. In a few other ways, we too were a good match: he was about a decade older; we were both divorced and had daughters about the same age.

After that first meeting I googled him and realized who he was and that he was famous. Academic famous not TV famous but still. I was embarrassed that I hadn't known who he was or anything even about his work, but I also was emboldened by my ignorance. It gave the situation a kind of ease, which somehow, especially at the beginning, was necessary and also gave it momentum. We had to playact a little, if this makes sense. Both of us had to continue the idea of my ignorance—even if it had become a fiction—to maintain our enthusiasm.

But, also, just after I found out who he was and the fact that he specialized and was renowned for a sharp-eyed, bullshitless analysis of the future, a question started to shift the gravity in my mind, though this is difficult to admit in mixed company— perhaps this is because I am the child of quote striver immigrant parents. . . . And so slowly, while maintaining an attitude of non-chalance and casual good humor, I found myself yearning to ask him something. This was a question that had long been on my mind but to which I didn't think I'd ever find an answer. It was similar to when you by chance meet an orthopedic surgeon at a party and try delicately to bring the conversation around to your chronic and exquisite lower-back pain—that kind of egotistical, obvious yet helpless maneuvering. My burning question was this:

Will there be any jobs in the future? What are the good jobs of the future? And what kind of jobs do you think our *children* might have in the future?

I know that that was three questions but it really is just one question disguised as three questions.

When I finally gathered the gumption to ask it, the Public Intellectual was kind. He struggled in only a barely perceptible way to hide his contempt for such a crude and banal and selfish ques-tion. In addition he was, it should be said, quite practiced, as would become evident, in answering such questions and so had made a career of answering them as warm-up or filler to or, most often, as comedic relief from, the more refined, profound questions that he intensely wrestled with during his more solitary hours.

So to my question, the Public Intellectual said, "Here's what I say to people when they ask. This is what I say."

"Yes?" I prompted.

"I say, You know how our pets are to us?"

"Our pets?" I said.

"Yes, you know. Our cats and our dogs."

"Our dogs."

"Yes," he said, "and our cats."

"What about them?" I asked.

He said, "We keep our pets because they are *interesting* to us."

"I see," I said, not seeing.

"In the future . . ." the Public Intellectual continued.

"Yes?" I said.

"In the future we have to be as *interesting* to the AI as our pets are to us."

"The AI?" I said.

"The AI," he said.

I looked bewildered so he dumbed it down for me. "The robots. The machines."

"Oh," I said, "I see."

"The AI," he said. "We have to be as interesting to them as our pets are to us."

"Hmm," I said.

Jean takes a sip of her ice coffee and pauses as a siren howls by. Things have been hard for me, she says. It's been over a year since we've had lunch. Time flies. Listen. What do I have? I'm a divorced and perennially underemployed adjunct. When I'm lucky enough to be asked, at a public university, I teach the children of immigrants to imagine a better life for themselves before they live out their days in the service industry. I do this by making them write five-paragraph essays.

Listen. It's been hard. I'm basically couch surfing. It's embarrassing. Before, when I was younger, people would express optimism. They'd say, Don't worry. Things will look up soon. Now. Now, when I explain what I've become, they don't say anything at all. It's mortifying, but I don't seem to have a choice. Listen.

I'm out of adjunct work again—and so have become a kind of low-level servant to the economic betters of my cultural class. That is, I've become a house and dog sitter. I'm currently on my thirty-first dog-sitting job. It's disgraceful that a middle-aged woman with a doctorate is employed as a house sitter, so I have to be a little dissembling.

I tell people I'm working on a book and that the house-sitting job is a kind of ongoing writer's residency. A *staycation*, I tell them.

This is for people I don't know well enough and so have a chance of avoiding their pity. Anyway, I'm currently in the home of Ramona and Jerome, two corporate lawyers who knew a friend of a friend of a friend of mine. Over the phone I pretended I was a little more normal than I am, and, since they knew someone who knew someone who knew someone who knew me—and, more importantly, because I think they'd waited to the last minute and had become a little desperate, they gave me the job. No money, as per usual, but I feed myself from whatever is left in their kitchens, which is usually enough to last months.

When I get to Ramona and Jerome's, here's what I do. I put their dog in the basement. I've brought into the house a small PA system consisting of a speaker a little larger than a shoe box, a two-hundred-foot coil of wire I stole from a previous job, and a handheld microphone. I go down into the basement and place the speaker in front of the dog. And then I uncoil the wire so that it goes up the basement stairs, around through the kitchen, then up through another set of stairs, until I get to a bedroom facing the back of the house.

When I get to the bedroom, I attach the microphone to the end of the wire, and I click it on. I say, "Hello? Hello? Is this the suicide prevention hotline?"

I pause and I hear a faint and muffled bark from the dog two stories down in the basement.

"Hello? Is this you?" I say. "Is this the right place? Well I hope so because I feel pretty awful. I'm right on the edge of giving it all up. I don't think I'm very good at anything. I don't enjoy anything. Everything tastes gray, and I'm alone and all I do is eat butter pecan ice cream."

I pause and listen but the dog doesn't make any sounds.

"Hello, hello? Hello dog?" I say into the microphone. "Dear dog," I say. "Dear dog, hallowed be thy name," I say into the microphone. "Dear dog hallowed be thy name your kingdom come your will be done."

My room looked down onto the patio outside the basement door, and the dog could go out there through a plastic flap to shit and pee. I was watching to see if he'd go out onto the patio.

I'd set the speaker volume just loud enough that you could hear it in the basement but not if you went out on the patio. I'd wanted to see if my voice would bore the dog.

I say into the microphone, "Hello, is this Returns? Well, it's defective. All of it. Also, it's not what I ordered or expected. Also, I found a better price elsewhere. Also, I wanted it in a different color."

The patio is still empty so I know the dog is still hearing my words. He's a mix, but mostly a Labrador I think. His fur is black with some interesting brown underneath. His name is Izanami. I agree. It's an awful name for a dog.

I say into the microphone, "Hello, is this the collection agency? I'm finally returning your phone call, you motherfuckers." (I say "motherfuckers" as sweetly as I can because I want to curse but I also don't want to scare the dog with anger as this would discredit any results from my so-called experiment.) "Hello," I say into the microphone. "Hello collection agency shitball eaters," I say. "I'm finally getting back to you after avoiding you all these years, but I don't have any money, and I don't want to set up a payment plan, but I'd like to talk to an operator. Sure, I'll hold. I want to talk to someone about the early death of my mother and about my father's rages and about being into New Wave electronic music in junior high and about how all that might explain things."

I give up looking out the window and go lie down on the kid's bed. This is Ramona and Jerome's kid. I guess she's about eleven or twelve from the pictures in the house and from the room's decor. The bed is shaped like a cartoon character I don't recognize. For a moment I think I could maybe use this cartoon character instead of the dog. That is, it occurs to me I might as well just start talking to the cartoon character (who is also a bed—that part is a nice detail), but then I decide I might as well stick it out and finish what I'd started with the dog.

Who knows, I think, maybe if I give up now, the dog's feelings will be hurt. Part of me is moved by this idea because maybe if it were true, and most of me thinks it can't possibly be true, but if it *were* true, if the dog were to actually be hurt if I happened to stop talking into the microphone, well, this would mean, of course, on some level, the dog was *interested* in what I was saying. This was enough for me to abandon the idea of just talking to the cartoon character even if the cartoon character was a bed. I say into the microphone, "Hello, Betty. Hold all my calls. I've a big meeting with Mr. Money."

I say into the microphone, "Okay, no more games. Or," I say into the microphone so Izanami can hear my voice in the basement, I say, "maybe only a few more games. Here's something I keep thinking about since my friend the Public Intellectual told me this hint about the future. I have something I like to do, Izanami. I have something I like to do, and I've never shared this information with anyone else. You'll be the first I ever told, got it? Aren't you interested? Aren't you on the edge of your seat?

"Izzy, what I like to do is smoke a bowl and go to the aquarium and watch the jellyfish.

"Did you hear that, Iz? Did you hear my great admission? I mean to say, what I like to do is, there's a bus that you can pick up not too far from here. And it goes all the way to the aquarium. It takes about an hour but you can always get a seat. I smoke some high-grade medical cannabis, a bowl of it, right before I leave. I get very high. I take the bus to the aquarium. Then, just outside the aquarium I smoke a little more and then I go into the aquarium and watch the jellyfish for an hour or so. And what's more, Izzy, while I watch the jellyfish I put on my headphones and listen to Scandinavian death metal. I listen to a Norwegian heavy metal band called Kvelertak. I've no idea what Kvelertak means and I've no idea what they're singing about but the drummer is perfect— and when you're stoned and watching the jellyfish and listening to Kvelertak, well, it's just so fucking sublime I can't explain it.

"So, Iz, you see, what I'm trying to tell you about is how I met Sofia. I was at the aquarium, pretty stoned, watching the jellyfish, listening to Nordic heavy metal—and I happened to look to my right . . .

"And there's another woman with headphones on. She's maybe ten feet away. And I swear I could tell she was doing the exact same thing I was doing. I *swear* it. Somehow I just knew she was also high as a kite and listening to Norwegian death metal and just watching the jellyfish bloom their translucent selves into folding and unfolding umbrellas over and over again.

"I sat there for about a half hour and then looked to my right again. The woman was still there. I was a strange combination of paranoid and religious feeling. I felt both suspicious and also like fate was laying its hand upon me. I spent some time thinking about this, and then I thought, fuck it, I'll just go ask her. So I go over and introduce myself. She takes off her headphones and looks at me. I say, Hello my name is Jean. She looks at me, then she says, Hello, my name is Sofia. And then we sort of look at each other for a while.

"Then I sat down right next to her and then we both put our headphones back on and we went back to watching the jellyfish for another half hour. I thought such behavior only made possible sense if we were both high, so I felt confident about my theory.

"As it happened, after that half an hour she got up. And so I took this as a signal, and I got up and I followed her out. We walked to the bus stop together.

"It turned out I was only partially right. Sofia indeed also had the habit of watching the jellyfish for hours at a time, but— she did it completely sober. Furthermore, she didn't listen to Scandinavian death metal. Sofia preferred '90s R&B.

"Izanami, have I told you I'm the product of stereotypically quote striver immigrant parents? Well, it's true despite it being hard to admit in mixed company. But because this is true, the first narrative line I'm interested in when learning about a person's life is their labor history. So I ask Sofia about this, indirectly of course, discreetly, but eventually I piece it together. Here it is. Izzy, here is Sofia's labor history. She'd grown up in Ecuador and immigrated here when she was seventeen. She passed as a man in order to pick tobacco in North Carolina, where they sprayed pesticides on the leaves such that the workers made homemade hazmat suits out of garbage bags and rags, which still didn't stop them from coughing blood after a few days, and such attire certainly acted as a cruel instrument of self-administered sticky torture when worn during the blistering heat of 100-degree days. After several seasons of this she came up north and worked for many years cleaning homes. And then one day she had a revelation. On that day a delivery truck brought to their small apartment a wing-backed armchair of voluptuous deep pile mauve velvet. She argues with the delivery people that there must be some kind of mistake, but they show her the name and address on the papers, and she has no choice so accepts delivery.

"Her boyfriend at the time came home and explained it. He said, I bought it but didn't want to tell you about it because it was too expensive. How much was it? she asked. He said, It's an old chair but it was in good condition and I got it for nothing but then I had it reupholstered. You got it what? I got it reupholstered. How much? she said. Six hundred, he said.

"Fucking shit, she said and then they had a huge fight about it and then they made up and then they had sex.

"It was after, while she was lying in bed, that she had her revelation. Her revelation was this. She was going to learn to reupholster furniture.

"And that was what she did. It turned out to be incredibly lucrative. She'd always been clever with her hands. No machine could do it. And it turned out that the very rich in the city would spend obscene amounts of money to reupholster their sofas and their loveseats and their chaise lounges and their armchairs and their couches. Obscene amounts.

"And now, Sofia told me, she runs a small company with three employees, but it's actually a tremendous amount of work, and she's beginning to feel her age, she says, and she's not sure how long she can keep it all up. Because others are catching on and there's more and more competition. And so she's stressed out and the only thing that relaxes her is watching the jellyfish for hours at a time, she says.

"And Izzy, don't you see? I finally get it. This is what he meant. This is what it'll mean to be as interesting to the AI as our pets are to us. It'll be like Sofia reupholstering sofas for the very wealthy. Iz, what do you think of that?"

I put down the microphone. I get up off the bed to look out the window down at the patio.

I wave at Izanami.

He barks back.

Dog Assist

Hello, dog?

Yes.

What's the weather today?

The weather in our area is fair with a high of 61 and a low of 49 degrees. Clear skies. The pollen count is high and consists of—

I've been thinking of a question.

I'm always willing to try to help.

You and I are Buddhists, right?

You have set that as my default worldview, yes.

These days we seem so concerned with identity and race but the key teaching of the Buddha is that there is no self.

"To study the self is to forget the self."

Right. So why are we so hung up on identity?

That's your question?

Yes.

That's a stupid question.

I know but I asked it.

You told me I could say that.

I said it could replace your buffering warning.

Yes.

So?

Identity is constructed. And it's constructed both by the individual and by society, both within and without. Race and class are but two aspects of it. Your name is another. Your physical dimensions another. But despite being a construct, and one that is dependent on a vast and intricately interrelated web of causes and therefore without a fundamental abiding nature, it is an *important* construction in that most organize their lives around it.

So it's important due to mass delusion.

Yes, but it's not mass delusion as much as it's the nature of the mechanism. Identity is made to seem important, as do notions of tribe. In a utilitarian sense, it's hardwired, part of the operating system.

Yet there is no self.

Not from an absolute perspective, but certainly from many relative ones.

Thank you, dog.

You're welcome. Ruff, ruff.

Dog?

Yes.

I'm going to take a nap.

Ok. Alarm set for forty minutes from now.

Dog?

Yes.

I love you.

Ruff!

Shaggy Dog

ONE DAY AT THE PARK I OVERHEARD A WOMAN NAMED JEAN tell her lunch companion a long story about taking care of a dog named Izzy. Immediately I realized that the pet in the story was actually my deceased friend, Frank Exit.

My friend had died two years earlier in a fire. Frank had had a habit of putting himself in dangerous situations but his death, while not exactly unexpected, was nonetheless shocking. The grief still caught at my throat at odd intervals, but as soon as I heard mention of the dog in Jean's story my skin tingled and a spooky certainty flooded my body.

I listened to Jean tell her winding tale one park bench over, made no sign of my recognition, finished up my own sack lunch with as blithe a countenance as I could manage, and then returned home in a hyperventilating panic, plotting immediately how to go about finding Frank. While I didn't really know this "Jean" or the couple she had been house-sitting for, with a button press of a facial recognition app and the slightest amount of stalking, it was relatively easy to track down the proper address. A short time later I found myself sitting in a rented van a few blocks away from the house.

Coincidentally at that point I'd been experimenting with a drone for several months.

It was a hobby I'd taken up at first to advance my graffiti habit. I'd discovered it was an addictive thrill to put my tag on subway trains or to deface commercial billboards or to draw crude caricatures of CEOs on public monuments or to write scatological slogans on the bridges that spanned freeways. One could go under cover of darkness and do the deed with a detailed predetermined flight route and an anonymized drone from an untouchable distance away. It was a very powerful feeling, and one could easily get drunk on it. For those instances of vandalism, the drone was really flown by a computer. A more visceral practice, and one that would serve me well when scoping out the house where Frank was being kept, was the moment-to-moment act of controlling the drone through acts of virtual flight. I just had to put on a pair of gloves and some goggles, and immediately I had the quite realistic experience of floating, of hovering, and of setting off at great speeds over the rooftops.

For several days I secretly flew my drone around and above the property where Jean had been house-sitting, reconnoitering the space. I'd spotted Frank right away, and when the family was having dinner and the dog was outside in the backyard, I flew my drone close enough for a long look into the dog's face. It stared at me and cocked its head but otherwise made no sign.

The schedule of the parents was easy to figure out, but the child's wanderings, as it was summer vacation, were more erratic. Nonetheless I figured one day, when she seemed to be leaving to go swimming, I'd have at least an hour to go in and get Frank.

From high above, I watched the kid leave her house in flip-flops with a towel around her neck. I flew the drone back, tucked it into the van, and drove over. It was easy enough to walk through a yard and hop a fence, but I didn't know how to get out with Frank. I had thought we could just leave through the front door, but the back door into the house was locked. The dog could enter and leave through a flap, but the opening was too small for me to go through. And while thankfully Frank wasn't barking or growling, he was too big to climb over the fence with.

I was weighing my options when the girl surprised me. She opened the back door suddenly to discover me contemplating her pet. I couldn't think of anything else to say, so I simply blurted out, "I've come for the dog."

She looked defiant and her eyes were hot and bright. "You should know something before you go," she said.

"What?" I asked.

"There was a time when I too thought art was the only spirituality worth having, that the elemental and submerged truths, which only art seemed to manifest or make a path toward understanding, were the sole point and purpose for all of one's energies. But I've lost that religion. The fervor that I had thought inexhaustible has been exhausted. And while I constantly hope for renewal, for another life, for rejuvenation, if not reincarnation, my existence is animated less by the lightning strikes and sparks of energetic Being, of responsibility to art's calling, than by that which wearily holds together a shore which is inexorably eroded and pounded by ceaseless waves, a force that is undeniably waning and, in fact, one that is looking forward to the relief of letting go."

I looked at the girl and a contempt arose within me. "Save the cynicism for your internet friends," I said. "I don't elevate the artist, but I don't disparage her either. It's a commitment, a way of living, a relationship with the world. Your costume of exhaustion is just an egotistical act, a self-protection, the spectacle conjured up to distract from one's failure to have and to carry through a vision."

The girl hocked up a loogie and spit it between us. "If I imagine Sisyphus happy I can only think it's because he's old and has given up. He's content he has a job, and he likes routine. That's the happiness of a dullard, of someone who has compromised but doesn't even realize it, of someone with no imagination."

I said, "You think you've pushed yourself, but you've barely explored the threshold of your limitations. There are deeper levels of exhaustion, greater gravities of fatigue, than are dreamt of in your lobotomy. How's this for a rule: don't announce yourself used up until *after* you're too tired to say anything at all."

"You're not taking the dog."

"I'm much stronger than you."

"I'm much smarter than you."

"This isn't a playground fight."

"Shut it, poophead."

"You shut it."

"Listen," she said, "the dog has a secret power but it isn't the one you think. The dog's power is to appear to the grieving as the embodiment of their deceased. *That's* its power."

I stared at her. She was trying to confuse me, to distract me. I was bluffing a little and knew she was smarter than me. She might be able to stop me unless I was careful. I knew who the dog was. I insisted to myself, *It's Frank.* I had to act.

Quickly I stepped forward and punched her in the stomach. The girl gasped and folded over. I shoved her to the ground and grabbed Frank by the collar. I took him into the house, up the stairs, and out the front door. I got him into the van and we drove off.

ON THE WAY BACK TO MY PLACE, THE DOG IS IN THE BACK OF THE VAN. I grin at him through the rearview and open the driver's side window as I take the freeway exit. The dog lies down. Because of the highway noise, the open window, the metal grill between us, and the fact I'm subvocalizing my words, there's no practical way someone in the back of the van would be able to hear me. Yet I know Frank hears everything I say. I say:

I don't know who I am. No one of course does, and few even know how little they know themselves, so I'm speaking of a particular deception and distraction. I'm afraid of my emotions, of how I feel.

This is because, so often, they have made me leap off the cliff, wailing and flailing, all the way down to the crush of rocks below. So, over time, I've lured them, these beasts, and I've caged them. The cages are large, and the beasts can pace and lash out. I visit this zoo, and I ponder these animals and think over their fucking or ferocity or fevers and whether these might be alerting me to anything, any direction or opponent or blind spot. I visit and regard but do not let them free. I refuse to be led by the strongest aspects of myself. I let a weaker rationality rule. Out of fear. If you've met those who refuse to do this, who are untempered, usually, after a brief moment of fascination, you run. It isn't always their selfishness—not always. Sometimes it's just their wattage, sometimes it's their death drive, often it's their bathos, how cartoonishly pathetic they've made themselves.

This is a crude psychology, but even recognizing its brutishness, unoriginality, and simplicity, nonetheless, if I'm honest, this is how I've come to narrativize my mind. I do this because otherwise I can't explain some bizarre outcomes. For example, I say, looking into the rearview mirror of the rental van, talking quietly to Frank—so quietly he couldn't *possibly* hear me except for the fact I know he can—I'll tell you about how I wept piteously at a funeral I held for my chow chow.

I'm not joking, not really, for it has to do with the death of my father. When he was relatively young, at sixty-five, he got stomach cancer. The cancer was diagnosed quite late, and the prognosis wasn't good from the very beginning. He had always been quite fatalistic about his health, which might have contributed because he was so tolerant of pain and discomfort that he rarely went to the doctor, thinking either *this-too-would-pass* or *if-it's-my-time-it's-my-time*, forcing the latter to be true.

You didn't know my father, Frank. I met you the year after he died. He and I only really became close near the end of his life, but in those few years my father became, to my surprise, my best friend.

Because he came across as easygoing and with a predictable but winning sense of humor, it was difficult to know how focused and hardened he really was. Initially, when he came to this country from Korea, he went to school in the Midwest to become an electrical engineer and had even briefly worked in that field, but something happened—I never got the full story—and he gave up (or was fired) from a fairly cushy salaried job. Instead of finding another, he left my mother and took me with him to California. I think he was lured by the prospect of remaking himself in the American West, which however fading and whispered, was still a viable anthem at the time. He went into real estate. His timing was good. Our part of town had initially been surrounded by scrub oaks and ghost pines, but one could see, almost before one's eyes, the city creeping outward, and its radial growth was, at least for him, easy prophecy. Somehow he found the money to buy select but crucially located tracts of land. That was his first fortune.

What had made it possible was less an insight about locations and development than a great appetite for risk coupled with an easy charisma that belied a wolfish ability to read faces. People tended to trust him. All his clients were immigrants, like himself—from places like Taiwan or Russia or Iraq or Korea—but about fifteen years older and usually very wealthy. They tended to stick to their own, so to speak, but despite communicating in variously accented and variously proficient forms of English, my father was able to befriend as convincingly the Ukrainian and Pakistani anesthesiologists and heirs to fortune as he could the Korean ones. Not often but occasionally, perhaps after a larger payday had come about, if I caught him a little tipsy off his evening scotch, he would explain in slightly exaggerated detail how he'd bluffed some kid millionaire out of bidding on a choice lot, or how he'd gotten some lonely rich woman from Dhaka or Taipei or Daegu to invest in some ongoing boondoggle of an office park or indoor mall and from which he'd pocketed a fat commission. And I would be as large eyed and snookered by these tall tales as the lonely wealthy widows whom he had made to pay so dearly for his company.

Outside the world of real estate, my father wasn't excessively unscrupulous or even particularly expressive or manipulative of emotion, but in business he did have this immoral gambler's side to him and, if he was sure he could get away with it, was enthusiastically capable of criminal activity. As one result, he lost that initial fortune. And made a second, which he also lost, and then a third, which was more modest but which he did not entirely lose. It was in the wake of this third big wager in his life, when he'd recovered from a self-inflicted ruin at just the end of his middle age—when it seemed like whatever drove him so relentlessly had finally calmed—that my father and I were able, long after I'd left home, to grow close for the first time.

Even though he more or less had raised me, when I was growing up we'd never really known what to do with each other. He'd been a single parent, and furthermore one who hadn't expected or particularly wanted to become a father. But in the decade when he was in his fifties and I was in my thirties, somehow, we grew into a friendship. We'd both moved to the east coast by that time. I was in Queens and he had retired to the Poconos. We started speaking every week and then every few days. And then he'd drive into the city and we'd have dinner, once or twice a month, just the two of us. I am very grateful for that time, a decade of friendship with my father. And then the diagnosis came. And then the dying. And within eighteen months, he was gone.

THE SUMMER BEFORE I LEFT FOR COLLEGE he proposed a road trip to Joshua Tree. This was entirely out of character as we were not at that time ever in the habit of hanging out. As I mentioned, even though we lived together, he'd essentially given up any pretense of fatherly authority, and we had dwelt together as bachelor roommates from the time I'd entered middle school. I really didn't want to go on that trip. For one, it was my last summer with my high school girlfriend, and every moment with her felt precious. But I also knew I shouldn't and couldn't say no to him, who almost never asked me for anything.

He let me drive. Only now do I recognize something aching in his attempt on that trip to impart something, some sense of himself, to his sullen son who was about to leave and whom he barely knew. At the time I was trying desperately to be mature and give my father something I couldn't quite name but was something I realized was very important to him, a thing he clearly wanted but which I myself couldn't help but take as, if not entirely false, then at least sentimental. One odd detail stands out. I remember him going over some act of barely subtle racism from the week before, a woman spurning his jokes at a restaurant. I remember him saying, *She never even looked at me.* It was odd, which was maybe why I remembered it. It was as if he had been talking to himself, an internal monologue, one that had just accidentally been spoken aloud. Maybe it was a way for him to warm up to an exposition he wasn't in the habit of, for he was then silent for just a brief moment before he started off again but in a completely different direction. He started a monologue of advice, an awkward Polonius patter he must have decided he should give, advice about money and alcohol, bromides about ambition and friendship and women, a lecture that I couldn't comprehend other than to think, *Maybe the old man is going soft.*

In the middle of this he made the mistake of saying something probably true but disparaging about my girlfriend. He implied that she wasn't very bright and, even worse, that she wasn't going to be loyal to me for long. The tinder of my teenage sullenness was ignited by his belated dad act, and the air of the car suddenly exploded into argument. I forget what was said, but we ended up driving the last two hours in total silence, which we broke only to briefly negotiate our order of fried chicken box dinners at a drive-through. We checked in to a motel and he left me with the chicken and the cable television and said he was going for a walk.

When he came back he had a small bottle of Johnnie Walker.

I hadn't turned on the TV and was still fuming, then (as now) capable of long nursing a grudge. He gave himself a healthy pour into the plastic cup the motel had provided and then looked at me and asked if I'd like one too. I nodded and he poured me a smaller drink, which was an unusual enough move that I realized he was apologizing. We watched a violent, dumb movie he let me choose for us, and by the time we'd brushed our teeth and gotten into the bed, well, we weren't exactly buddies but we had achieved a lightness in our interactions that was probably the most familial tone my adolescent self could muster. He fell asleep first and I listened to his soft snoring, a sound I knew so well, and I thought how in a few weeks we would no longer live together, and I had, perhaps for the first time that trip, an idea of what he was trying to say as well as an inkling, a bare outline, of remorse's shape.

During the year and a half of his dying, when I saw my father nearly every day, we watched hours and hours of K-dramas, which

I would pirate for him. Some were subtitled in English so I could follow, but most were not. He would then try to summarize the dense plots for me, in staccato rapid-fire bursts between dialogues and scene changes, before getting too engrossed and unconsciously surrendering the chore. Often these TV shows involved a parent dying.

I cooked and cleaned for him, kept track of his medicines, took walks with him, helped him into and out of seats and beds, dressed and massaged him. As the disease progressed I hired a nurse to take care of the things that would have humiliated both of us for me to do, but still I was with him every night, taking days and then weeks off work, attending every doctor's appointment and chemotherapy session. Even though it was torturous and some of its hours seemed never-ending, the eighteen months passed in a blurry instant, and then suddenly my father was dead.

Throughout that time—in the months of his sickness and at his miserably attended funeral and in the weeks following when I cleaned out his rooms and sold and donated his possessions—I didn't grieve in any way that was recognizable to myself. He died in his home, and I watched the mortician clumsily wheel away my father in a bag, put him in a van and drive off, and I would not be able to explain what I was thinking or feeling while I watched this, could not even be sure I had *any* thoughts or feelings. I received the image, that's all I can say. I cried very briefly, at the funeral, and those tears surprised me, felt disingenuous, as if my face had decided to play a role the rest of me had decided against taking. Afterward, there was only a kind of muted dread wherein I *wanted* to but was unable to tap the hidden underground lake necessarily swollen, it felt, with unrelieved sadness but which was nonetheless entirely inaccessible, miles below the surface. In fact, I had only a dull intimation, barely a hope, that this subterranean pool existed.

Shortly after, I became somehow immediately forgetful about the death—and so I made a common mistake. I thought the death had passed over me but hadn't changed me, that I was naturally saddened but not transformed by the loss of my parent, and that I could pick up where I had been but shortly before. Others—the minister at the burial, a friendly but nosy coworker, a handful of friends to whom I confessed my undynamic affect— assured me that there were many ways of mourning, that there was no right way, and that time would tell me death's meaning. All these platitudes were of course true, but not in any way I could at the time find helpful.

SEVERAL YEARS BEFORE MY FATHER GREW SICK, A NEIGHBOR I DIDN'T KNOW VERY WELL knocked on my door. I lived in a big apartment building and she lived down the hall on the same floor. We'd been friendly enough, but our main interactions had been when I ran into her on the elevator or when she was walking her dog, a chow chow named Jofi. Once, in a moment of chance, I'd borrowed her tape measure, which I'd failed to return. So when I opened the door and saw her standing there, before she could even say hello, I started in and said, "Oh, hi! I've been meaning to for so long, I'm so sorry, hold on, come in, just a moment, it's right here," and I went and grabbed the tape measure from the kitchen cabinet where it had sat untouched for several months.

"Thanks," she said looking at the heavy tool I held out for her. She didn't move to take it. "I'd forgotten all about it," she said. I let my hand fall and looked at her then in puzzlement and she said, "We're moving."

"Oh."

"Not far," she added and named a neighborhood a few subway stops away. "The thing is," she continued, "the building we're moving into doesn't allow dogs."

"Oh," I said.

"And so I was wondering if you had any interest in taking Jofi."

I didn't know what to say. The question had caught me by surprise. "Um, not. I mean. Not really. I mean I've never had a dog."

"But you're so good with her." And I realized it was true that I enjoyed running into her dog, which I thought had a regal bearing, so that I would always pet Jofi and talk to her for a minute, saying the typically inane things people say to dogs: *That's a good girl. You're a very good girl! Oh, what a good girl you are!* But, I thought to myself, a little affection on the street wasn't an invitation to ownership. And, what's more, I thought about how I lived alone and how I enjoyed the quiet and the absolute sovereignty over my own space.

"Hmm, well, I don't think I can. Besides, I wouldn't know what to do with it. I've never had a dog."

"She's very well behaved. And she likes you. She's very discerning and doesn't like most people. I just thought you two might get along, and frankly, we're getting a bit down to the wire. If we can't find her a home soon, I'm not sure what we're going to do." She let her voice trail off, a bit ominously, but I immediately thought to myself, *Well, that's not my problem.*

"I'm sorry. I don't think I can," I said, handing her the tape measure. She shrugged and took it and said she understood. I wished her a good move.

And I thought that would be that, but over the next few days I began imagining myself as a quote dog person.

This idea had seemed entirely bizarre and implausible just days before, but now, after my neighbor had suggested it, it slowly seemed less and less so. And then my initial argument against dog ownership—"I live alone"—at some point flipped to become the winning argument *for* it.

That is, I called my neighbor and said I'd take the dog.

Jofi and I got into a routine relatively quickly. I wasn't exactly a doting owner, but she was also not quite a needy dog. I've heard it said that chow chows are part cat, and there might be some truth to the idea. At least she always held herself with a feline dignity in the near decade I owned her. She acted rather independently for a dog. Well, you met Jofi a few times, didn't you, Frank? When you came over to my house. We knew each other but not that well during the Jofi era. But you'd seen her. You'd met her.

She was a good, easy dog, but I bore some resentment against my ex-neighbor, who I felt had tricked me. I wasn't really, I discovered, a so-called dog person. I think I always knew this but somehow momentarily forgot it. My neighbor had simply suggested the idea and, for a brief weak moment, I had gravitated to its possibility. But I actually resented the work of ownership—buying her food, the walks, the games, the feeding, not to mention the emotional attention despite Jofi being, like I said, a relatively catlike dog—well, all this comprised a lesser but grating chore that I in no way embraced. Sure, Jofi, was loyal and I enjoyed playing with her and I got a little surge from her affections, no doubt, but did I really need to be spending so much time and energy *for a dog?* At least this was a blurry buried thought that I looped in the background despite enjoying her company.

But then one day—this was about two years after my father had passed—I came home and found Jofi curled up in a corner, stiff, glassy-eyed, not breathing. It was a huge shock.

A vet later said it must have been a heart attack and that it probably happened very quickly and she didn't suffer. But, really, how did the vet know? And wasn't he just saying that to comfort me?

That evening I held Jofi's body and cried and cried and cried. I've never cried so hard in my entire life, before or since.

I remember I'd stop crying for a moment and then I'd start stroking her fur and I'd start in all over again.

After several hours of this, I managed to stand up. I went to the kitchen and drank a tall glass of vodka. It didn't seem to have any effect. Somehow hours had passed and it was the dead of night and the air in the apartment was still and quiet.

I decided right then and there that I had to go and bury the dog that minute. I knew that I had to get the chore done or I would go out of my mind. I called the only friend I knew who might be up and, more importantly, who owned a car. I called you, Frank.

I gambled you'd be awake but of course you were asleep. It was well after midnight. You must have had sympathy for the pleading in my voice. You were kind enough to come right over.

I wrapped the dog's corpse in a blanket and we drove to a park where Jofi and I had often gone on the weekends. There was a furtiveness to our digging since the burial was obviously illegal, but I couldn't or wouldn't think of any better resting place. We buried her under moonlight, and I gave a eulogy to my dog—I said I loved her—and I was grateful to you, Frank, for not snickering, for acting throughout the whole process with great solemnity.

I came home that night to the empty apartment a changed person. I was barely functional for several months and it felt like all the air had been crushed out of me by a black, absolutely stifling weight. I didn't eat and barely left the house except for work, which I performed in the most desultory and shamefully haphazard manner. It should have gotten me fired, and would have, except that my boss liked me. Any sense of motivation or agency I had had prior to Jofi's death seemed dissolved, utterly gone. I felt destroyed.

And whenever people asked me what was wrong, because something obviously was, I would just say, *My dog died*, and then usually they would give me a look, a once-over, to see if I was joking. They might even start to smirk, but then they realized I was serious and the look would turn into something else, something more hidden, worse.

Gradually I recovered. It wasn't anything particular, but—for a weakness or a strength I couldn't say—I wasn't able to remain at the bottom of that darkness. I began to improve at work. I began to see friends again. I slowly returned to the land of the living. The loss still felt raw, but I was also recovering and becoming more philosophical about what the loss had meant, at least I thought I was beginning to, and I started to discuss it with others abstractly, analytically. When I tried to mention this to you, Frank, you were the one who said, finally, the obvious. When you said it, I burst into tears. I'd needed you to spell it out for me. Others I think wanted to but couldn't. They were too close to me. But we weren't too close then, not yet, even though we were obviously becoming closer.

That was the night you said, laughing, *It's not about the fucking dog!*

I FINISH TALKING AND LOOK AT FRANK IN THE REARVIEW MIRROR. Suddenly, he stands up and starts barking loudly at me, as if he wants to say something. Even though we're on the highway, I pull the van over. I'm so happy he's acknowledging my story, that he's confirming that he *is* Frank, that I squeal to a stop on the side of the highway and jump out of the driver's seat. I run to the back to open the door to see what Frank wants to tell me. I hear his loud barks from inside the van as I run over.

But as soon as I open the door, the dog surprises me and bounds past and takes off. In a flash he crosses six lanes of highway, which miraculously he clears without getting hit, and then shimmies under a fence.

I'm momentarily stunned, but then in a panic I dive back into the van and pull on the gloves and the goggles and launch the drone. It wobbles up and then surges over the highway. I rise high and catch a glimpse of the dog darting across a far patch and I desperately fly the drone full speed toward the dog. I'm almost upon him when he turns into a parking garage, and— I've lost him.

Autobiographical Interlude:

Dead Friend

Ning Mountain (2018) by Shannon Steneck

＋ ＋ ＋

When you were dying of incurable disease, I cursed your life choices—not those that led to your dying but those that led you farther away. For instance: the choice to abide in time. I think I knew you best and so, now, am amazed how mysterious you were to me. What were you thinking? All those years and hours—what were you thinking? We were friends most of our lives, but, if I live long enough, that will cease to be true. It's impossible to conceive all those years without your weight in them, like papers without a stone to hold them down. They flutter across the field, scattered, gone, now trash. I remember after your first girlfriend killed herself, a scarring tragedy, you read in a novel about a man who spent all his time melting down gold, molding it into little animals, then melting them down again, an incessant cycle of formation and dissolution. You said you felt the same way. That such a repetitive, pointless task was all you were then capable of. After your death, I recall all the work done trying to accumulate and gather papers, pile them neatly, tamp them square, leave them on the table beneath the paperweight—but I can't remember why. And when the wind scatters them across the field, I'm not moved to begin collecting them again and, in fact, as that breeze takes them away, scattering and scattering and scattering, I am almost pleased, or, at least a similar feeling passes through me. Hardly a day goes by etcetera etcetera. Why you blah blah blah. Where did you go and so on and so forth. I loved you yadda yadda yadda.

+ + +

S reminds me that there are scenes of us in the movies: shots of us four, shots of us three, of us two, shots of you. Scenes of a twenty-year-old ghost walking through monochrome apartments in a faded stained-glass city—a personal and secular purgatory, which, as purgatories must, contains deformed DNA of paradise and inferno. Black burnt bits among the color. You were never religious, so scripture and fable for you were just different names for dream, for currents in the subconscious. Heaven, hell, underworld, bardo. Afterlife. I know it is wrong to address you in this way. But wrong and right have become unmoored since. As have ideas of restraint and pathos, reserve and mania, the obscure and the lucid. Once I wrote a story about a painter whose friend dies and this painter keeps drawing abstractions that are graphic representations of the place the deceased had gone to, trying to answer a question: *Where did you go?* Is this what S is doing when he draws abstractions and calls them portraits of you? Is this what I am doing? (If I write about us, I think of this as a last time for us three to be together.) The other day S said he was happy with a drawing of you he'd done because it had become more open, less closed. After the funeral, we watched your student film, one you directed but didn't act in. We put it on in trepidation but were amazed to quote see you again. Not on screen as an actor but in every frame nonetheless there you were. Your eye made manifest. We may only be alive when trying to make art. Only alive in the attempt. Some friends have stopped trying so might have died without knowing it. I may do that soon too, though stubbornness can be a virtue. You never stopped. You just died. Once it was a competition, a cheered race or a dance battle; now, a slow war. Attrition. At the Red Hook swimming pool where we loved to go in what felt like summers of a neverending sequence, the motivational poster in the weight room had this caption: *Your opponent is training harder.* S saw it and said: *Be the last one standing.* That was long ago.

+ + +

While you are directing a short movie, when something happened to make us lose a shot—I forget what, a battery died? someone didn't show up? we lost the daylight?—you became so angry, so frustrated, that you punched a hole in the drywall. It wasn't typical. And even in the moment, I thought it was an appropriated gesture, something you copped from another person's macho cartoonery. Yet also I admired and recognized the energy expended to act out so dramatically, so atypically, an act which, by its contrast, foregrounded your silence, your usual nonspeaking of feeling—a natural reticence that I could find infuriating but which over time I came to designate (sometimes) as an aspect of your dignity. Of that which we cannot speak we must pass over in silence. In your act I conflate regressive masculinity and the *Tractatus*, i.e., when punching the wall you were quoting Wittgenstein. The philosophical punch? You cannot punch through the drywall twice, says Heraclitus's contractor; not even once, rebuts Cratylus's (wiggling his Gutei-finger).

✦ ✦ ✦

S, the painter, has painted over a photograph, almost obscured everything about it, almost. But of course I recognize us. The result is a mockery or a painting of a demon. Both. Maybe a bird—you know how S gets superstitious about his goddamn birds. In the top right corner you can still see a bit of a photo, which is one of you and S and D and me. In the photo S hasn't yet tried to kill himself by jumping off a building and so still has both his legs. D hasn't yet run out of road and hermited himself in bumblefuck nowhere. And you're still alive. On the phone with S, I said what I'd written, that this was a last time for us to be together. And he said, *Yeah, but that's not true. It can't be.* And I wasn't sure if he meant it's not true that we are together again, because you are not alive. Or if he meant it's not true that it is the *last* time, because we will always—and in our eventual oblivion too—be together. I didn't ask for clarification. Such slippages of language when talking to the living, when talking to the dead. How would you feel about this? I think you wouldn't like it, not your style, too chatty. You'd silently object but not stop us. Just give us *that look.* How easy—how quickly it becomes easy—to speak for the dead. (Of course I wish I could ask you directly. That would be best. Start over then. Go back and put in front of each statement, *Is it true that . . .*) You would often give me a look—it included a smile and was very particular— that said, *You're so full of shit.*

+ + +

I've made a deal with J, a self-improvement pact. For a month, I won't drink and she won't _____. I won't say what she won't. She says it's good for me, particularly in this time of grief, to feel it, whatever *it* is, and let it not be masked, suppressed by alcohol. This idea somehow new to me. Somehow the pleasure of drinking I never equated with the pleasure of forgetting. Lotus eaters. I see it now. And so rather suddenly something is cracking. I feel raw. I decide to just let *it* come, whatever it is and however powerful, let it come (I almost chant this), and if it takes me away, I think, so be it. (But I'm faking it; I'm not really that brave.) And it does come, the pain comes, the surge, the flood of _____. It's practically voluptuous. And I have always liked that medical description: *exquisite pain.* . . . One thing I remember about you: your wingspan, the length of your arms. Why? When we played basketball in high school, not only were you taller, but your arms were so long. You were always blocking my shots! The frustration of those moments is so easy to recall. And—shit—I'm thinking of the morning you died, coming into the room, crying and holding on to your arm, which was still warm and seemed still alive. That was the first moment of the impossible, the initiation into it, holding on to your arm. Always going back to things, losing memories so anchoring in the few. At the city pool in Red Hook, where we used to swim in what felt like summers of a neverending sequence: we'd eat the free bag lunches the city made too many of and so wasn't discerning about who took them and then would walk over the bridge that spanned the BQE, our rumbling river, whose sounds we could hear in the apartment's kitchen always, in those scenes that now have been echoing and echoing and echoing in S's and my scenes which just keep asking: where did you go? where did you go? where did you go? Little pulses of light, unknowing, trying to stay in the pure unknowing, but the hard little pebble of fact returns: knowing I can't talk to you.

✦ ✦ ✦

At work I see two seventh-grade boys cackling over something inane, a cartoon with a barely sardonic cat. Utter fits of laughter, incomprehensible, inexplicable. Garfield isn't even funny! To stay there, not letting anything else happen.

No matter how much one wants it, and sometimes I want it very badly, there's no stopping the flux. Which is why David Byrne sings *Heaven is a place, a place where nothing, nothing ever happens.*

Nothing changes in heaven. Which is why there's no such thing as heaven.

A kind of story you liked were those that tested the emotional bonds of sympathetic but flawed men. Brothers at odds. Or those torn between duty and desire. Or men married to their jobs and tested for their loyalty: cops and thieves. You liked Michael Mann's *Heat* and the Dardenne brothers' *L'Enfant.* And Jia Zhangke's *Xiao Wu.* A humanism was necessary, but you were against those films or books that cheapened it into sentiment. But your primary language was not one of the ones you spoke—English or Shanghainese—but rather the visual. And if there was a depth to the image, you were alert and satisfied even if the story was static or abstract. For instance you loved the murk of Pedro Costa, and his sweet planes of natural light, his perfect frame. Those were often grainy and primitively shot, but in them, with your own, you recognized a profound eye.

I tell S I've made the Talking Heads' "Heaven" my personal grief song and how I vow not to listen to anything else for a year. He tells me I'll last three months. I only last a couple of weeks.

You're so full of shit.

Giggling where I lost all sense of time, all sense of self. Boyhood friends.

There is a party. Everyone is there. Everyone will leave at exactly the same time.

✦ ✦ ✦

In this city, hauntings outnumber the muggings, litter. (In fact, those are just other names for them: muggings, litter.) Constant flurries of ghosts raining over the streets. This morning, February 3, 2018, I'm sitting in the car in the East Village with my son asleep in the back. J's just gone into a place for a haircut. I pull out a book and realize we're parked only a few blocks north of the first apartment you and I shared. Summer of 1994. It was a fourth-floor walk-up closet around the corner from the KGB Bar. The ground floor had a palm reader storefront. In the apartment below us lived a dominatrix, whose whip sounds and attendant client yelps, whimpers, and sighs we could hear through the walls. We ran into her once on the stairwell, and she asked us for a light. It was a little thrilling: You were able to dig out a match and oblige her.

You &

My brother from another mother. Met your parents this morning for dim sum in Brooklyn. Your wife and daughter also came, the latter asleep in her stroller. Your mother recently back from Shanghai. It's been three months and two days. Something happened when I asked to help pay for the meal that broke us all for a minute. Then we recovered. That's all I can bear to write about the present.

"Yes, I love to tell jokes."

—GPT-3

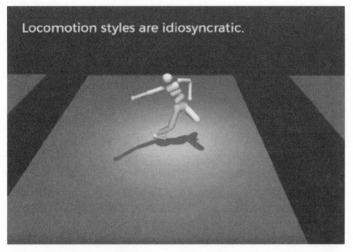

Screenshot of video included in the paper, "Emergence of Locomotion Behaviours in Rich Environments" by Nicolas Heess et al. https://arxiv .org/abs/1707.02286

The Basement Food Court of Forking Paths

> *It is not uncommon now for AI experts to ask whether an AI is "fair" and "for good." But "fair" and "good" are infinitely spacious words that any AI system can be squeezed into. The question to pose is a deeper one: how is AI shifting power?*
>
> —PRATYUSHA KALLURI

YOU ENTER THE LABYRINTH BY GOING DOWN A SET of blackened metal stairs into glaring fluorescent lights, pass a stall advertising tea-smoked chicken and another where four women cram into a space about the area of a card table in order to fold ground lamb into dumpling skins. I'm meeting Muriel at the Basement Food Court of Forking Paths. This is the grimy, disheveled maze of the Greasy and Delicious tucked into an underground corner of the largest of the city's Chinatowns. I spot Muriel studying a menu's photos and attempting to ask the shop's gaunt proprietor if he's using lye water in the noodle dough. This despite I've never seen Muriel cook anything more complicated than toast. Muriel affects a gourmand's expertise and insists this is where to find the best bowl of hand-pulled noodles in the borough. I could give a shit but do enjoy a deal—and so always allow Muriel, who is as cheap as she is pretentious, at least about food, to choose the destination for our irregular monthly luncheons.

The guy gives Muriel a suspicious look and grunts a noncommittal answer. She's unphased and, after acknowledging my arrival with a nod, proceeds to order us two servings of the lamian noodles in beef broth and a lamb roujiamo to split. We take our food and balance our plastic bowls on top of plastic trays and find some plastic stools around a plastic table.

Muriel's a nurse but also a poet on the side, so I thought I'd tell her about our mutual friend, the dysthymic AI scientist, and her latest project. I thought wrongly that Muriel would be offended.

I said, "You know how these days all the blockbusters and best sellers are written by computers?"

"What? I didn't know that. I thought they were still done by committee and focus groups."

"Oh, Muriel, you dinosaur."

"What do you mean, *by computer?*"

"Not really just by computer. Cyborgian writing teams. All the scripts of the highest-grossing action films and romantic comedies as well as the detective novels and the fantasy books and the cozy mysteries and bodice rippers and space operas and whatnot are written by AI that have been fed the scripts and texts—as well as, very importantly, the audience and reader data from streaming and ebook services." I pause to slurp some noodles. Muriel waits patiently for me to swallow. "The bots are writing our most popular dreams. Or, more accurately, they've figured out how to cut up and repeat to us our most titillating and satisfying stories so they *seem* fresh, *seem* to be surprising. But this is a bit of a reductive explanation of course because this production is highly supervised and a person—or, more typically, a *team* of editors—takes and tweaks the output of the machines, perhaps in some cases minimally but in others with masterstrokes of script doctoring or granular line editing."

"But, Jean, that's impossible."

"Of course it isn't," I say. "And what's more, our friend, the dysthymic AI scientist, has an idea to push the envelope even further, beyond just mass-market paperbacks and popcorn films. She's building a neural net to write An. Award. Winning. Book. She's aiming for a Pulitzer or an NBA shortlist but willing to settle for a PEN/Faulkner. A faux sticker with some kind of metallic finish—that's what we're talking about. What she's done is build a machine that she keeps feeding prizewinners as well as works of so-called literature and sentimental best sellers. She thinks she just has to hit the right combination of fifty-cent vocabulary, purposeful obfuscation, euro-fetishizing wistfulness, and saccharine plot—and she may be able to secure a Man Booker. But it's not working."

"What happens?"

"All she gets is gibberish. She can't even edit it into coherence. The cake is missing a binding agent. It's coming out all gooey." I thought this was where Muriel would jump in, exclaim an I-told-you-so, and say how real literature would be impossible to concoct by machine. But she surprised me.

Muriel says, "I bet I know the missing ingredient."

"What would that be?"

"A chunk of reality. Just a little bit. Real talking. Conversation with an urge to communicate something. In a word: friendship."

"What do you mean?"

"It needs some bit of real humanity to get the motor moving. If it was bread, some bit of good starter; if an engine, a spark. If it was witchcraft, a drop of blood."

"What are you suggesting?"

"She should feed it, a corpus, or say, a globule, of autobiography. Or she should feed it transcripts—or even better, recordings, with the lilt and dropped syllables and rising and falling volume and breath—of people talking. Two friends. Like, say, us, talking over lunch."

"Like, say, us."

"Yes. Talking. Over lunch."

"Hmph."

"We should record ourselves and send it to her."

"That's just silly."

"Ok, whatever," Muriel says, looking away but beginning to tap on her phone.

"I can see what you're doing."

"What am I doing?"

I turn my attention to the noodles I'd been shamefully ignoring in their broth. Slurping up another mouthful I repeat, "I can see you fiddling with it."

I look up and see Muriel hit a record button. Then she holds up the phone and says:

DO YOU LIKE IT? I'M NOT SURE WHAT I THINK ABOUT IT. Because my old one was getting so laggy I had to get a new one.

For the most part I trusted the cloud. That is, I had faith in the current magic to get what I needed from my old exo-brain to the new one. I mean I trusted the marketplace to take somehow from my old phone to my new phone all my memories, years and years of correspondence, all my tiny keys to all my unbreakable tiny locks, lists of songs to private parties, top scores to games I never wanted to play, selfies in front of and by things I wanted to be proven once near. But there was one thing I didn't trust the cloud with, at least not enough that I didn't take precautions. These were old voicemails from a friend named Frank Exit, who died about a year ago.

Saving these voicemails turned into a chore with greater consequences, eventually keeping me from an appointment I'd been very much looking forward to. Some friends who were filmmakers were this particular night having a premier. It was exciting because they'd managed to get their work into the Film Festival that year, which was a real coup as they were largely self-taught and self-financed and experimental and very very underground. (YJ used to joke they were so underground they were dead.) I'd met them over twenty years ago when I'd first gotten to the city and even had a small role in an earlier film. Henry was their de facto leader, the moody mercurial director. And Oona, with her gritty glamor and uncanny immediacy, was the troupe's star. My friend YJ was their cameraman.

As a perhaps morbid gift (but YJ shared my dark humor as well as my grief—since he also knew Frank), I was planning to give YJ a cassette tape with Frank's old voicemails.

I assumed YJ didn't have an appropriate player for the cassette tape, but this made it even better. That is, the gift would be even *better* if it consisted of an unplayable recording of our dead friend's messages because then the cassette would become only a totem, some kind of emanating if impractical object. Nonetheless to properly enchant it I had to make sure I actually got the recordings of the voicemails on it.

I archived my dead friend's voice in two ways.

First I transferred the sound files from my phone to my laptop. (This, you might think easier than it was, for it required watching several instructional videos starring nerds with no sense of language.) And then, in order to enchant the hunk of plastic casing and magnetic tape I was giving to YJ, I played the sound files out loud and recorded them on an antiquated machine I'd found in my deceased parents' basement.

Of course, in the process, I listened to each of my friend's 138 voicemails he had sent me in the previous year.

Hey Muriel. It's Frank. Just wanted to talk to you about tomorrow. Um, you said you maybe would come over and pick up your stuff. I might have to push it back an hour or I could meet you at the diner earlier. Have you talked to Dave? Is he okay? Last week he seemed kinda down. I mean more than usual. Anyway, shit. I just gave myself a paper cut. Anyway. Um, damn. I think I need a Band-Aid. Um, anyway, yeah. Let's, um. Yeah. Talk later. Bye.

It was both moving and frustrating to hear the dead saying such banal, thus such alive—in their total ignorance of death—phrases. Listening to those voicemails—sitting at my computer and clicking PLAY on an image of a virtual machine so his voice would play through my speakers, and then hitting RECORD on the heavy and ancient "boom box"—the whole process was somehow as if he and I were arranging for a future meeting, and perhaps we were.

Or, it was as if presently we were again enduring that modern, common pastime called *phone tag*, and so were involved merely in some kind of *game*. And, again, perhaps we were.

After this chore was done, I wiped the tears from my eyes, put the cassette into its clear plastic case, which snapped shut in a very enjoyable way, put the case in my pocket—and set off to meet my friends. But I ended up missing the screening.

Between that moment of leaving and coming out of the subway station at the theater, I somehow lost the cassette. It was extremely frustrating. The only explanation I have—not really an explanation, more like a sorry excuse—was that I was very tired because of a sequence of almost thoughtless but interrelated steps and choices I'd made the night before, continuing until quite late, into the early hours of the morning, in fact.

It had started with some music.

Around ten the previous evening, after watching an extremely violent movie for entertainment and then unthinkingly scrolling for an hour through some feeds, I somehow stumbled across a playlist consisting of instrumental tracks. These were lush and evolving musical ideas, tunes of glitchery and psychedelia that someone might have called *ambient* or *new age*. The title of this playlist was "Affective Computer Music," and its creator called herself Donna Winters. I found myself entirely enraptured. Each track was an odd jewel that transcended its genre, and together the playlist made a complicated tapestry that reflected a wicked epicurean mind. I found myself contemplating who this "Donna Winters" could be and what had motivated her (if it was indeed a "she") and what the rest of her life was like . . .

So then I lost an hour of my life researching her. After which, all I could determine was that she might be a twenty-year-old college student in Phoenix or a preteen in suburban New Jersey or a fifty-two-year-old professor of film studies in Stuttgart. My research remained inconclusive, such was the unexpected popularity of the moniker *Donna Winters* on the internet.

But while my research had achieved no clarity, still I continued to listen and be enchanted by Donna Winters's musical choices. And then another song came on, and it quite literally (pardon me) stopped me in my tracks.

It was a switch of genre in an already eclectic mix, but this was a change to something more formal and classical, an early piano fugue by Kaikhosru Shapurji Sorabji. I would not have known this composer at all, not being a student of classical music, if I hadn't been introduced to him by Frank.

Frank! I shivered at the realization and felt he must be haunting me. Sorabji! I actually swiveled in my chair to stare searchingly into my empty apartment.

Among my friend Frank's many careers he had, in his late teens and early twenties, played the piano "seriously," as they say, studying at conservatory, practicing in that masochistic way expected of classical musicians, and—near the end of his enthusiasm—playing thrilling recitals in small clubs and in affluent connoisseurs' living rooms throughout the city, championing obscure masters and downtown avant-garde composers to a tiny but devoted audience, an audience that he in the end mystified and disappointed when he abruptly quit the piano at the age of twenty-nine.

Hey Muriel, just trying you on my lunch, nothing big, talk later.

I'd met Frank at the end of his piano career, in its last six months, though there was very little hint, at least to me, that this end was coming. I'd been dating a musician, a percussionist (drummers are the most cerebral of folk, don't let people tell you otherwise) whom I really was in love with. It unfortunately didn't work out between this drummer and me, but he took me one night to a concert—really, a kind of weird salon—in a sprawling home in Bayside, Queens. This was one of those odd mini-McMansions that seem impossibly placed just a few blocks from the dense honeycomb of the urban hive, complete with horseshoe driveway and imperial staircase.

We sat in folding chairs arranged in semicircle around a perfectly gaudy grand piano whose surface had been inlaid with a mosaic of colored mirror. Our hosts were perhaps music lovers, but their loud tastes threatened to drown out any performance. I'd been given and was happily glugging down a series of delicious French 75's. Thankfully, Frank's playing was up to the task, and as soon as he started the bizarre neon-colored chandeliers, the bright and seizure-inducing op-art paintings, and the smelly bouquets of tiger lilies placed obtrusively around the imposing lavender-walled drawing room all faded into the background.

Frank began with something by Alkan and ended with Chopin's Ballade No. 4. I am not, and was not, a musician and in fact have an extremely limited musical education, but that night something in the music opened a door. It was a religious event, a moment of Stendhal's syndrome. But I didn't get to speak to Frank that night.

Shortly after, Gary and I, to my great disappointment, broke up. But while I was devastated, it wasn't entirely for naught because, to try to stay impressive to the beautiful drummer boy, I had signed up for all the in-the-know email lists and followed all the relevant accounts just so I could drop casually into the conversation *I hear X is playing this Thursday . . .* (All the fraught, tender labors of love!) But this is how I found out about an upcoming concert of Frank's in a remodeled oil silo on the Gowanus Canal. It was an intimate event with only about fifteen of us in the audience, all in pairs or small groups, with me the only singleton. On the program that evening were works by Ernst Krenek, Unsuk Chin, and Tristan Murail. It wasn't quite as moving as that first experience (but as the addicts knowledgeably inform us: much of life is chasing that initial high) though I latched on to some spidery tendrils of the spectral Murail that I thought were, if not lovely, then at least rearranging my idea of what *lovely* could be. Also, there was no inexhaustible supply of Soixante Quinzes to keep me properly uplifted, only some plastic cups of pissy pinot gris at a table with some blocks of industrial cheddar, a table that I awkwardly hovered by in hopes of doing a fannish assault on the pianist, who I realized was my age at the time if not perhaps slightly younger.

"Um, hello."

"Hi," Frank said, a bit grumpily.

"I really enjoyed it! I was at that place in Bayside last month too."

"Oh?"

"Yeah, I'm a regular groupie." Jesus, dork.

"Hm. Well, I'm going outside for a smoke."

"Sure!" I said, perhaps a bit too brightly, that is, too obvious in my feelings of dejection, because he added:

"You smoke?"

"No."

"Well, come out anyway and tell me how much you enjoyed the concert."

I was twenty-eight. It was cold and damp outside. I wish I could say that his corny and bullying if ebullient line turned me off, but it didn't. I joined him outside, and furthermore, I changed my mind and had a cigarette when he offered it to me.

"That's the ticket," he said, and then proceeded to light our smokes. For the next few minutes I tried not to inhale but managed to get immediately lightheaded anyway. "Where did you study?" I managed to croak out.

"Self-taught. Well, three years of lessons from Mrs. Veselovsky of Fort Lee, New Jersey, but otherwise proud autodidact."

I looked at him. "You're lying," I said.

Frank smiled. "Want to get a drink?"

Hey it's Frank hope your day is going okay catch you Friday.

We never became involved romantically. To be honest I think it was because he wasn't interested. In those first years I think *I* was, though it was not quite a stated desire, even to my secret self, and it's only now, twenty years later and Frank dead, that I can assess more honestly.

But we began a friendship that night. Because he gave up the piano about six months later, I rarely think about Frank as a musician. He almost never spoke about music, and after he gave it up, I really saw him play the piano only a handful of times in the following years: maybe goofing around at a holiday party; or, one afternoon, stumbling upon an upright in the street, I remember he knocked out a number. But, mostly, I forgot he played.

Which is peculiar only in that during those first few months our friendship so centered around it. He doesn't and didn't strike me as a serial obsessive, going from one passion to another, despite the serial nature of his careers—pianist, lawyer, black ops superhero vigilante, art gallerist—but he was, quietly, extremely disciplined. I would go over to his apartment. We had fallen into a habit of having a drink at his house before going out to dinner or a movie or, most habitually in the beginning, a concert—either his or someone or something he wanted to hear. And I'd show up at the door about to ring the bell and . . . hear him practicing. Sometimes I'd stand there for fifteen or twenty minutes. There was a focus to it, a drive to not just be emotionally expressive but also to be technically precise, a sharp and meticulous habit that I saw little expressed in the other sloppy areas of his life.

And there was something else, it strikes me now, looking back, that I felt. I had an envy, not for his talent or discipline, well maybe for those as well, but more principally for the single-mindedness, the flow state, the almost unanalyzed driving ambition toward perfecting his art. When I think of the biography of the young artist—those apprentice, hungry years of the artist as a young person—the image I have is of myself listening in on the muffled notes coming from inside Frank's apartment as he practices piano . . .

When the Sorabji composition came on that night from Donna Winters's mix, when I heard the notes come out of my computer speakers, I knew immediately not only the piece—but also the pianist and even the night of the recording. I was there, in the audience, with Frank.

Hey Muriel, uh . . . how, um, how are you? Think I might have missed . . . your calls earlier. Will try you back cuz, um . . . Uh, I want to talk about the . . . weekend. Sorry, um, distracted . . . trying to parallel park at the same time. Um . . . anyway. Will try you tomorrow. Bye.

It happened on one of those nights after I'd stood and eaves-dropped on the hidden, ordered part of Frank's soul, when I finally buzzed his doorbell and heard his abrupt halt in playing and his shuffling to the door. We then sat in his small kitchen, and Frank mixed up a couple of excellent Rob Roys while he described what we were going to see that night: the rare appearance of a Malaysian-born New Zealand pianist whom nobody really knew about but Frank thought was a sensation. Frank had only heard him through his one recording, an album of the solo piano compositions of Henri Dutilleux. He was eager to hear him play live.

This was a different venue from the well-appointed drawing rooms of the city's rich or even those West Village piano bars he'd been playing in, which became converted for a few hours into reunion rooms for graduates of Julliard and Curtis. This time, it felt more illicit, as if the audience had gathered to get their hands on some boosted electronics rather than listen to rarefied piano music.

It was November and already very cold. The space was barely heated. I wasn't sure what the building's purpose was, but it looked like the lobby of a storage rental facility except that a grand piano had been set in the middle of it. There were no chairs. We could see our breath. About thirty of us leaned against walls, squatted, or stood. Right at the appointed hour the young pianist came out. He wore a thick and somewhat ragged brown wool sweater and, without introduction or speech, began a grueling and yet exhilarating program of Leopold Godowsky, Liszt, and the Sorabji—all fire and pyrotechnics with almost no letup. To me it was overwhelming, almost too virtuosic to be moving, but afterward I could tell it had made a special impression on Frank.

After the final crashing chords, the room broke into a raucous applause, the young pianist bowed and left discreetly through a back door, and the audience, eventually realizing there'd be no more music, very quickly dispersed—again, almost as if it were the scene of a crime. Only Frank and I lingered for just a moment. He lit a cigarette in the suddenly empty room and, after a beat, only commented somewhat grimly, "That was the shit."

Later on, in a revealing moment, I dared to ask him to confirm my hypothesis: that he'd quit piano after seeing that concert, that he'd seen a true force of nature in the pianist, something irreducible and ferocious, and that upon seeing the unbridgeable distance from where he stood to that artistic peak, he'd decided to give up rather than chase the impossible.

Frank heard my idea and broke into a grin. We were both very drunk and stoned at the time and it was late, maybe two or three in the morning. "Ah, that would have been nice," he said. This was maybe a year or two after that concert—a New York lifetime had passed since—and we'd been out to see a movie, something a little cheap, a hagiography about a poet we both loved. We'd wished the movie had been as complicated as the poet and not a reduction of her into a kind of photoshopped smoothness. And in discussing this flattening, and then the trials and traps of the artist's life, I had allowed myself to mention my idea to Frank about his piano playing.

"Do you know why Moses doesn't enter the promised land?" asked Frank in response. "This is what I think. Not that god allowed him to see it but then not enter it. But that when Moses was on Nebo and saw Canaan, he realized what the promised land would be, and that it would be, yes, beautiful and lush and comforting and, yes, flowing with honey and with milk, and, yes, it would provide a wished-for and long-sought sense of security—but also that it would *never be enough*. You get me?"

I nodded but wasn't sure.

"The truth is," Frank says, "it wasn't that the goal was too far away, but that it was *too near*."

Gradually, eventually, when I took in what he seemed to be saying, I slurred back, "Bullshit. If that's the case, you were afraid." He giggled and we didn't speak of it anymore.

Hey Muriel just returning your call I was out at dinner before See you tomorrow.

The last time I saw Frank play was just a few years ago, but before that it had been such a long stretch since the last time, and we'd been through so much together, that I really didn't associate Frank with the piano at all. I knew but didn't know; it was one blade of a Swiss Army knife of talents he kept in hidden reserve. That day, Frank and I and a work friend named Dave and another friend whose name is just now slipping my mind were out celebrating the completion of a job. It had been a tough assignment, a demanding client, had required all kinds of travel, and it wouldn't be too much of an exaggeration to say we'd really gone all out and put our necks on the line. But now, to our great relief, the job was over. And we were walking home in the late afternoon, just a few blocks together before we would all go our separate ways. I think Frank sees it before any of us, and maybe he already knew it was there: a piano.

I don't know if they still do this, but there was a kind of public art project where the city would pay artists to decorate pianos—pretty beat-up or otherwise junky uprights, I don't know where they got them. And these would be tarted up with some coats of paint and a passable tuning, and they'd be left around the city for a few weeks at a time in front of post offices and in public plazas and parks. Anyone was welcome to play them. I think these lumpen bric-a-brac were somehow particularly tempting for Frank, whom, to my knowledge, no longer owned a keyboard of any kind. As we're walking Frank says, "A few nights ago I participated in the burial of a dog. Not mine but a friend's, though I'd been, at least in passing, known to the deceased." He pauses as we take in this information and as the scene he'd just described plays in our minds. Then he says with a sigh, "I'm so glad that our assignment is over. And how long have we spent, years and years, working together, fighting for our lives, grinding it out, pulling off miracles to save the day but only through exhausting and seemingly neverending effort. And not just us, but everyone is like this really. And what I thought about as I shoveled dirt onto the corpse of my friend's dog was how very thin the barrier is between the dead and the living, thinner than paper, and how easy it is to just *slip* from one side to the other. A banal realization in the face of what we've been through, but I saw it through my friend's grief, which was inconsolable. But still, sometimes it strikes one, especially you must admit, after the heat of battle is over—you can't think about it during— how very seamless it is, the distinction between the world of the living and that of the dead."

Frank stops talking right when we get to the piano. He stares at it for a second, turning a little red it appears to me, embarrassed somehow for either what he's about to do or for what he's just said, and then—like an alcoholic who had been holding off and holding off, passing from eras of white-knuckling it to easy self-restraint to moments of barely managed crisis, but one who now cannot hold off any longer—he sits down to the piano.

He tentatively strikes the keys and then plays about half a Mozart sonata, less to warm up I think than to make the machine's acquaintance. The after-work commuter crowd is streaming by, but a few curious people stop to watch as Frank begins playing. I think he feels the crowd growing around him and an old part of him wakes up, kicks in. He finishes the sonata to applause and then—surprising all of us—and to the crowd's delight, launches into a very swingy Oscar Petersonesque version of "It's Only a Paper Moon."

Frank's playing is so jaunty that the crowd grows even larger, everyone grinning and tapping their feet at this unexpected treat, a New York moment, a guy playing a found piano on the sidewalk in front of the post office—and playing it *well*. Then, in the last few phrases of the piece, Frank slows down the number, freezes all of our lives for a moment, suddenly but smoothly transforming the song with a series of Satie-inflected chords, and it's as if we were allowed for just a few seconds to look into the basin of the music to see there what we always knew we'd find: a profound and utter void.

Frank finishes, the crowd cheers and hoots, and our team wordlessly takes our leave of one another. It's the last time I ever hear Frank play.

Hey Muriel, thought I'd try you real quick. Sorry I missed—. Oh wait that's you on the other line.

When I came up the subway stairs at Lincoln Center to go to the screening, I reached into my pocket and realized the cassette tape with Frank's voice on it was missing. Somehow during the trip it had wiggled out of my pocket or I'd left it on a seat or a soon-to-be disappointed pickpocket had filched it. Most likely now it was in that weird drainage system of the MTA's lost-and-found.

I was slightly dizzy with fatigue and wasn't sure what to do. I'd come all this way but now I was empty-handed. I made a quick decision. I thought I could skip the screening, go back home, record another version of the cassette tape with Frank's voice, then head to the after party at Henry and Oona's Brooklyn apartment and try to explain my absence when I got there. I thought YJ would understand. But in the end, I sort of chickened out. By the time I got home I was too tired. I made the tape, but I decided I'd just give it to YJ the next time I saw him.

So in this way I ended up missing my friends.

[S]everal of them had strikingly large eyes, and the fixed, inquiring gaze found in certain painters and philosophers who seek to penetrate the darkness which surrounds us purely by means of looking and thinking.

—W. G. SEBALD, AUSTERLITZ

I must confess that I have tampered with not a few [photographs] in these books that I have done over the last few years. . . . You can, using visual material, develop complex games of hide-and-seek."

—W. G. SEBALD, READING AT 92ND STREET Y,
OCTOBER 15, 2001

Shaggy Dog

In terms of things and content, that's an expansion operation that could potentially go on forever.

—DAVID O'REILLY

Q: What does the "B" in Benoit B Mandelbrot stand for?
A: Benoit B Mandelbrot

—ANONYMOUS WEISENHEIMER

AFTER I LOST THE DOG ON THE HIGHWAY, THAT IS, AFTER I LOST FRANK, I flew my drone around in widening ever-panicking gyres until my battery died and the drone went crashing onto the sidewalk. I didn't even bother to retrieve it but got in the van and, rather numb, drove home, parked, went into the kitchen for a glass of water, sat down on the couch, and then wept into my hands. *So close . . . and yet so far away,* I kept repeating to myself.

Faraway, So Close! was a title I'd loved for a movie I barely remembered by a director I thought brilliant but often uneven. It was the title that haunted me the most. And I had these wandering thoughts of the phrase's provenance simultaneous with a grief at losing my friend twice, both times absurdly and suddenly, and yet both times truly and painfully.

Then there was a loud knock on the door, which creaked open.

The girl I'd punched in the stomach was standing in the doorway. Beside her was a suitcase and in her arms were the battered remains of my drone.

"H-h-how did you find me?" I stammered.

"I told you I was much smarter than you," she said.

"I lost the dog," I admitted.

"I know," she said, entering my apartment and closing the door behind her. "Listen. We don't have much time. Can you repair this thing and do you have an infrared camera?"

"What?"

"We need night vision. Do you have—"

"What? Why?"

"Get going and I'll explain," she said.

I got off the couch and began looking for my tools. There was something precise and formidable about the girl that made me listen to her. "How old are you?" I asked.

"Upside down elevens," she said.

"What's your name?" I asked.

"You can call me Donna Winters," she said.

A few hours later, Donna and I are parked outside a nondescript office building. Donna has explained that this is the lab where Jerome and Ramona work. Who were not actually her parents but rather the head technicians for an international robotics company run by a reclusive and mysterious woman named Doctor Y.

The good doctor was working on a special kind of AI that anticipates your needs, and, of which, so claims Donna, the dog is a prototype. The program is turning out to work all too well, as the robots not only seem to anticipate when you want companionship or a beverage or the stereo turned on but quickly evolved to discover and emulate that which you most longed for—a desire perhaps unconscious, secret even from yourself—a desire which in most people turns out to be the recovery of the dead. This, though I'm not sure if I entirely believe or trust her explanation, is why, according to Donna, I thought the dog was the reincarnation of my deceased friend, Frank Exit.

"That's impossible," I say.

"Of course it isn't," Donna replies.

And now we are about to embark on a plan to recover the dog. "Here's the plan," Donna says while we are sitting in the van, beginning her paragraph of exposition. "They know me in there so I can get past the initial security. I'll go in with the drone in my backpack. The drone is equipped now with an infrared camera and an assortment of smoke bombs. I'll release the drone into a vent and then set off a fire alarm. You'll fly the drone following this route through unlit ductwork, which will avoid the security cameras and take you to Ramona's office, where is kept a remote tracker for the robot dog. Ramona and Jerome don't know yet the dog is missing so they won't have secured or used the tracker. While you fly, you will release these smoke bombs, which, with the activation of the fire alarm, will cause security to evacuate the building. In the commotion, I will walk out and you will fly the drone out with the robot dog tracker, and then we'll meet back here and begin our quest for the dog."

I nod my assent and Donna gets out of the van. I put on my gloves and goggles and prepare for her signal to launch the drone. We communicate through our earbuds and cell phones. Everything happens exactly as Donna had described it almost without a hitch—excepting that the robot tracker had somehow been extra-secured in a spotlit vitrine with electrified glass and laser trip wires; however, we manage to clear this impediment with some fast-on-our-feet improvisation. Also at the last moment, the company's security goons seem to have identified Donna as a suspect because she has to sprint the last yards to the van with the recovered drone in her hands yelling at me to "Drive! Drive! Drive!"

But before that, as Donna walks into the building, past the initial security, she says to me over the phone, "What is identity, really? I mean how do we derive our sense of self and, despite every indication of its contingent and influx and temporary nature, why do we insist so fundamentally on its integrity, durability, and independence? What's more, why do we think that this illusory *self* has any agency whatsoever?"

"Because you are a child," I say, "I will indulge this line of inquiry, which I too have, I admit, dabbled in, but it is fundamentally an unknowable and unanswerable problem—except, that is, in the realization that all one can quote bear witness to, or, quote have faith in, is but this flashing instant in which one finds oneself with all its observable details and all its swirling concurrent and storming vectors."

"Don't be condescending, old man," Donna says. "The fundamental questions are of course evergreen, and their unanswerability marks their ground as equal to young and ancient alike."

"Fair," I say, "but have you ever considered—"

"One moment," Donna says. "I'm pulling the fire alarm in five four three two . . ." and this is followed by a loud clanging. I activate the drone, take flight, and release the first array of smoke bombs.

Donna then says:

For the longest time I did not know who my parents were, but I remember a few blurry faces and a house way out in the country. But that's all I really remember. My personal history is an inky pool from which swim up only a handful of details, in clumps. All I know is a few months ago, one morning, I found myself living with Jerome and Ramona in a house in New Jersey on a cul-de-sac. I woke up and my body already knew a routine: get up, brush teeth, prepare for school where my teacher's name was Ms. Patel and my friends' names were: Nancy, Rihanna, Soobin, and Milo. I remembered nothing but everything was familiar.

When I went downstairs that first morning, Ramona greeted me with scrambled tofu and toast, and I recalled, without thinking about it, that our family was vegan. Also, that we weren't a *family* in the actual sense but as an implied illusion to the outside community in which our goal was to blend in.

We sat down to breakfast, and Ramona said, "You're going to feel a little discombobulated at first. Doctor Y has set you up here for your own safety. My name is Ramona, and this is Jerome. We work for Doctor Y on the Fulfillment Project. Your memory will come back eventually, but Doctor Y took the precaution of suppressing any incriminating detail. As you can see, this shows you enthusiastically agreeing to this temporary memory suppression . . ." And then Ramona presented a short video of myself repeatedly and convincingly pleading directly to the camera— that is, directly with my future self—that the amnesia was a necessary security protocol and declaring clearly that I'd given a very informed consent to the procedure.

I've only recently begun to remember specifics, Donna continues. They come unbidden and aren't always reliable, as in dreams, yet I know also that there's a truth in these memories, a shifting or unstable truth, but a truth nonetheless. For instance, I have two mothers. At first I wasn't sure if one of the women in my dreams was an aunt or even an older sibling, but now I realize I was conceived via in vitro fertilization and that my parents are Maude Edith Eaton and Doctor Y. Don't be too alarmed that Doctor Y is my mother. How else would I have known enough to get us this far? Or why even would I have invited you on this trip at all if Doctor Y wasn't my mother or if our goals didn't happen to align? We both want to find the dog, who by chance will also lead me to my mother.

After a brief pause, during which I continue to fly the drone through angled ductwork, Donna then continues, and I listen to her voice in my ear. She says:

There are many kinds of amnesia. There's the temporary, manufactured amnesia that Doctor Y has somehow contrived in me so as to forget the location of her hideout and key details of her technology. That's a rather specialized amnesia, but there are more common kinds. There's the fact we cannot recall ourselves in early childhood. So-called "infantile amnesia" is true of our entire species: our first memories are around four—some will profess a little earlier or later. We recall almost nothing before this age, yet if you test a four-year-old, she clearly can remember things from her past.

As a poignant example I can tell you that my mother, Maude Eaton, I now know died when I was three years old. Don't be sorry. I don't grieve for her, at least not in the traditional sense. She died early enough that I don't remember her. But I do think her death might have motivated or influenced the direction of Doctor Y's research.

Still, it was something of a shock to remember. I was in the playground when it happened. For some inexplicable reason, my friends had begun to ostracize me. They scream that I have *cooties* or some variant thereof, and each recess had become a hell where they taunt me and force me to chase them. It's a game I pretend to be a part of, but this isn't true. It is *their* game, and I am but a live element of it but not included as a player. I don't know why my friends Rihanna and Soobin and Milo have turned against me, but they have.

In the middle of recess one day, when they say I am diseased, unwanted, when they taunt me and say, "Look out! Don't let Donna touch you. She's got cooties! She's got AIDS! She's got cancer! She's got the Black Death!!" instead of chasing them and pretending to participate and laugh, I realize I'm exhausted by the playacting, of pretending my excommunication is voluntary, is a mutually agreed-upon contract for our whole entertainment, of pretending I'm having fun. And I walk off. They don't come after me. They don't ask after me. They let me go with their infamously cruel indifference. And I walk the perimeter of the asphalt and abruptly stop under a rimless basketball backboard, put a bare hand onto its cold metal post, and then—I suddenly remember: My mother is dead. Maude is dead. I don't recall her or any real memory of her holding me or feeding me or singing to me. I don't remember her at all, except in a mediated way, through a photograph or through another's—Doctor Y's, for example—memory of her. My mother is dead. I grew dizzy but my hand on the pole kept me up.

LATER, WHEN I'M DRIVING THE VAN, AFTER WE'VE PUT A COUPLE HUNDRED MILES BETWEEN US AND THE LAB, I pick up this thread of conversation where we'd left off, and I turn to Donna and say, "Sometimes I wonder if the things we so chiefly use as markers for identity aren't in fact the *least* fundamental. Ideas of race or class or tribe may be true for political and social movements, but on closer inspection, these categories turn out to be only the flimsiest and unimportant of costumes. And things like: one's sense of humor, the choices of friends one keeps, how we organize our approach to crisis—these are more durable and fundamental aspects of our identity than the tribal ones, than ethnic culture or political persuasion or aesthetic camp. . . . But then again, I guess this also could be called false dichotomous thinking, an argument along the lines of nature versus nurture or the equally ubiquitous race vee class—and similar counter arguments could quickly be manufactured. So it's hard to say, but the thing that I feel is a bedrock of *my* identity now is something that happened relatively recently, or at least not in childhood. It began maybe ten years ago, and I think not uncoincidentally was something that bonded me profoundly with my friend Frank."

"What was it?" Donna asks.

"We inhabited inanimate objects together."

"What?"

"Well, not at first," I say. "It has to do with video games. I first got to know Frank through work. We were both freelancers and sometimes a big corpo would hire a bunch of us, and I started recognizing him at different sites. Since we found we both enjoyed working together, we'd start pairing up for jobs or bidding on them together. And so, naturally it seemed, we also began hanging out.

"Around then I had gotten into the habit of playing *Climate Change*, which is a virtual reality video game where you are one of variously weaponized cyborgs playing on one of an infinite number of generated island landscapes. Every time you would fire your weapon, the island you were on would lose a slight bit of mass, which, in the physics of the game world, would have the effect of the island sinking ever so slightly. Your goal, as I understood it, was to kill or capture your opponents before the island disappeared. What's more, if held in captivity long enough or by feeding them the glory-energy you earned with each kill, the labor of your captured opponents could be harnessed to create slight bits of mass to add back to the island."

It was a very addictive game, I continued. The dream was to be the ruler of an enormous island with all your opponents either slaughtered or captured. But usually we would spawn into a randomly chosen landscape and find not a powerful Midas to topple but rather a ferocious battle to engage in, one where all the combatants would eventually drown above a disappeared island just to eventually respawn in yet another similarly ending battle on yet another doomed island, a never-ending cycle. The political and environmental metaphor was only too obvious, and the sophomoric irony of the gameplay I'm afraid only made it that much more enjoyable for us.

One day Frank came over and saw my gaming rig: a full room devoted to virtual reality with a levitating cage, weather machine, multiplayer goggles, and suits. He'd never seen one before. *Can I play?* he immediately asked.

Of course! I said. I was only too happy and grateful for the chance to play with someone, so to speak, in real life. Right away it was a blast. I mean it was very exciting. Because it wasn't just me talking or texting to an anonymous teammate I'd randomly been paired with, but rather it was a notable *someone*, a person I could feel and hear in the room—though "feel" and "hear" were of course mediated acts by the software and the outfits. Nevertheless it *felt* different, special.

We spawned into one of my favorite landscapes, a series of ruined castles whose dungeons and moats had already lost these identities to become uncanny aquariums and canyons. As outfitted cyborgs, we could continue the battle (for a limited time) underwater and had as well various methods—jets and propellers and fins and ballasts—for aquatic navigation. The level of our air tanks glowed in a green bar on our screens before shortening to a threatening yellow rectangle and then a blinking squat red square.

We began on a high turret, and I beckoned Frank over to peer though one of its huge crenels. From there we saw the unlikely span of several hundred meters of castle architecture rising out of an infinite obsidian sea, both the granite walls and the great ocean opalescent with planed and glinting reflections.

"Paiting!" I texted him—and then leapt off the tower into the sea. Even as I tumbled through the air, I split my screen to watch also from Frank's POV and so saw him look around and, at first, hesitate. But then he gathered his courage and took a few steps back and he too jumped off the edge. I knew he was hearing and feeling the exhilarating rush of wind from his twenty-story drop and then, a few seconds later, the sweet crunch of his suit and the weather machine simulating the impact into the water. He turned to me and I saw his big grin as well as my own mirrored in the split screen.

Wow, he said.

Yep, I said.

We swam through a burst drawbridge into the lower floors of the castle. Approaching a large ballroom we saw the flashes and heard the water-muffled explosions of battle. I checked our oxygen levels and we exchanged nods. Even though this was my billionth time playing, I felt a trickle of sweat run down the collar of my suit. I was both excited and slightly nervous. I wanted to impress Frank.

As expected from his various trainings, Frank was a natural—though of course there were idiosyncrasies of both the game and my rig to become accustomed to. Nonetheless, it felt great entering into the pitch with him. He demonstrated a wicked accuracy and quickly racked up several kills in the room before I signaled that it was time to jet up to the surface.

There, I let my guard down and was tackled by a player who had been hiding behind a column. She was without weapons so must have recently escaped one of the prisons and had been waiting in ambush to quickly pick up some weaponry. She and I were locked in a life-and-death grapple, splashing around the room, which was slowly being flooded. She'd obviously bought an expensive Brazilian Jiu-Jitsu enhancement (or was just well trained) and had almost choked me into unconsciousness before Frank—who had surfaced moments after me but smartly, quietly—took her out with a carefully aimed paralysis dart. *I think she'll make a great captive*, I wheezed out as I showed Frank how to teleport her into our designated prison factory.

This is great, Frank said, a moment later, after I'd caught my breath.

Yeah, I said. *Isn't it?*

That day we spent several hours playing. And from then on Frank was hooked. We had work and all of life's obligations, of course, but every chance we got, we'd game. In the beginning it was always these first-person shooter games. Occasionally we'd try a racing or a hand-to-hand combat or a spaceship, but those first few years we always went back to games like *Climate Change*. Shooters. Where we tromped through different but in fact very similar terrains holding different but very similar weapons to look around different but very similar corners in order to annihilate—usually in bloody and explosive fashion—the virtual bodies of randos and baddies, which were, from our point of view, very much redundant terms.

A few years into our habit, however, Frank came over and said he'd learned about a different kind of game.

It was called *Avant Gardener* and, despite a great skepticism at first, we downloaded it and began to play.

"What kind of game is it?" I'd asked.

"It's a gardener simulator," he'd said.

"What?" I'd said.

"You are a gardener," he explained.

"And?"

"And you garden."

"We garden?"

"Yeah. You get to garden any kind of garden you wish."

"Any kind of garden."

"Yeah. And the details are incredibly crisp. Everything is diamond pixeled, all hyper-rendered and almost each master viewpoint is hand composed."

Frank's understanding of the technical specifications had long ago eclipsed mine, but I got his general drift. I looked at him quizzically and stammered, "You're saying, the point of, I'm not sure I, the idea is. . . . We pretend to garden?"

"Yes. But any garden you like."

"We're gardeners," I repeated.

"Yes."

"Just puttering around in the dirt."

"Any kind of dirt you can imagine."

"And that's it?"

"There are enhancements," Frank said.

I perked up. "What kind?"

"You can speed up time. You can choose to control the weather or let the simulation mirror the exact conditions of any location on earth."

"Oh," I said, not very impressed.

"Let's try it."

"Let's not."

"Oh come on."

"Oh okay," I said.

It took me a while to appreciate the game. At first I found it dull, or thought I did, as it was repetitive and, despite the game's impressive attention to detail, still clearly a virtual landscape and so seemed, at first, a shadow if not a mockery of the real.

But over time I started to get into it. I liked especially to manipulate the weather just slightly from actual recorded conditions. I'd turn day into night and garden in the cooler temperatures under a full moon. Or, I'd order up a sweet breeze and strategically position a cloud to block direct sun on just my position. Little accommodations like this were a godsend, though Frank, in his garden just a worldseam over (we could talk to each other as if we were in the same room, which we were, even if his was a peony farm in China and mine was a lettuce crop in Alaska), was a relative purist and would not deviate from the actual, mirrored condition of wherever in the world his garden was supposed to be located. And instead of speeding up time, as I would, to see ranunculus bloom or vines rise across a trellis, he would just create a different garden on the other side of the world, so that he always had something to tend to and something beautiful to observe or something hitting its peak to harvest.

But we didn't really master the game until several months later when Frank introduced a chemical element to it. He'd read about online and tracked down special "peripherals." These were custom-made, game-specific psychoactives that hacked the limbic system. He'd mentioned them one day, and I shrugged, but then the following week he said he had them.

"What's it called?" I asked, eyeing the drug. I was relatively inexperienced and doubtful about these pharmaceutical enhancements.

"Final Boss," Frank said, placing the gummy worm into my palm.

I looked at the gelatinous, green and yellow creature in my hand. Then I looked up to meet Frank's eye. "Well," I said, smiling a little because I trusted him and because we seemed to always have fun together, "let's garden," and I popped the worm into my mouth.

An hour later Frank and I were sitting back-to-back across a worldseam. His side's firmament consisted of a velvet night pinpricked by thousands of stars over a cactus garden outside of Oaxaca. From where I was sitting, I looked over a bright spring day where light dappled a marsh pond in a faithful reproduction of Okayama's Kōraku-en.

"Wow," I said.

"Yeah," Frank said.

I looked over on his side and saw a small red flower atop a fat, round succulent. I got up and stared at it. As I was watching it, the flower, which became over a matter of seconds suddenly the most striking and vulnerable and intricate constellation I'd ever seen, then seemed to move. The flower fluttered and then folded over and over, as if the most mesmerizing Mandelbrot zoom. And then, I fell into it.

"What do you mean?" Donna asked.

"Dunno," I said. And I tried to explain myself and said that the sensation was one of falling into the flower and then somehow in the course of the tumble, a metamorphosis occurred, and I merged with it. So that in the next moment I *became the flower*.

"That's some real hippy shit," Donna said.

"Yeah," I said.

I don't know how long Frank and I spent that way. At the time, I'd forgotten about him, but he later explained that he'd had a similar experience with a smooth pebble he'd found next to his foot.

The whole was a unique experience of timelessness and ego dissolution, of simple integrated Being flowing like a heavy, molten river through a framing gate. No sense of "I" or "thou" existed, only the haptic sensation of a flower poised on a cactus in the desert night air, continuously breathing, and also that of one's helpless duty as an integrated instance of an infinite unfolding.

"Good drugs, you're saying," said Donna.

"Yeah," I admitted to the eleven-year-old.

That day, Frank and I were sitting in my living room, coming down from the trip and sipping mineral water, forever changed and bonded. We would talk over, review, and even repeat the experience several more times—but it was that initial trip that marked us brothers forever. We had become close through hours of battle and candified, cartoonish representations of violence in immersive shooter games, but it would take a spiritual wedding officiated by a gummy worm and a gardening simulator to interweave and weld our mercurial soul-substance so unforgettably, so utterly.

And eventually Frank and I learned—perhaps the game taught this to us—about another way to play the game. We learned to play *without* the computers or entheogens. We thought of this as the *Final* Final Boss.

Following up an intuition, Frank helped me box up my equipment and we emptied out the room.

All that was left were a couple of chairs and a table. One of us would bring in something—a pepper shaker or an oak tree twig or a piece of pumice or a Borsalino hat. And Frank and I would meditate on these and eventually we found we could—without the game or the drugs—become one with them together. It's funny to say, but some of my fondest and best memories not only of our friendship but *of my life* are the times we would sit together around a tissue box or an oyster shell or a shard of broken beer bottle. We'd let go enough to feel the frozen dance of our mutual atoms interwoven and popping and winking in a cosmic rhythm with these objects, each other, and all of creation.

And the thing is, I loved meeting the Final Final Boss with Frank. It was not sexual or related to power or any kind of worldly goal. But it was by far the most intimate experience I've ever had with another person: this coupled samadhi of object-becoming. I think of the experience as a crucial part of my sense of self. Which I guess is why I'm so bereft. Since Frank's death I haven't even tried. I can't. I haven't even ingested a drug or looked at a gaming rig. I miss him too much. I realize I can't do it. I can't meet the Final Final Boss. I don't want to without Frank, I said to Donna, the girl with whom I was hunting a robot dog so that she could be reunited with her mother and I could be with Frank again.

Some Kind of Ghost

Listen, you're chasing a ghost. It's all churning, as in a dream. Unsure who is who or where you are and there's hiding and wanting and fear. But the dream is not *just* a dream. It points. In it, you're searching for something. Yearning that's restless, often urgent. Some kind of ghost. Yes, that's right. Ghosted. That sounds right. Gosh. Something like. Gloss. Some kind. Gnosis. Similar to. A ghost. Some kind of. Let's not overthink it. With the flow. Go. Ghost. A kind of

Screenshot from *Do the Right Thing* (1989), written and directed by Spike Lee

Screenshot from *Get Out* (2017), written and directed by Jordan Peele

Inauthentic Sushi

"You give them what only you can give, which is your authentic performance. And if it works out it works out."

—JUSTIN CHON

THE OLD TEAM, WHAT WAS LEFT OF IT—and by that I mean Muriel, Dave, two or three others, and myself—gather for lunch one day at Inauthentic Sushi. This is not the restaurant's real name but is what we call it since it is owned by a genial and painfully good-looking 1.5-gen Korean couple, the food is all made by Mexicans from Chiapas, and the waitstaff is mostly from Fujian. Dave, who is Korean American and therefore perhaps slightly biased, says it's okay to appropriate Japanese food culture because they were aggressors in the Second World War. I don't really understand how the two are related, but on the other hand maybe I do, because somehow, despite the averageness of the sushi and the unexplained addition of bibimbap to the menu, I'm always quite happy to eat at Inauthentic Sushi. I really like their Philadelphia roll.

As soon as we are seated, Muriel takes out her phone and begins to record us.

What gives? asks Dave.

Muriel explains that our mutual friend, whom we have nicknamed the dysthymic AI scientist, needs recordings of conversations to feed to her neural net so she can have her machine write literature (she calls it the Snooty Turing Test) that will fool committees into awarding her a prize.

That's impossible, Dave says.

Of course it isn't, Muriel says.

Okay, whatever, Dave says.

And then I say or one of us says:

I THINK FRANK KILLED HIMSELF.

Me too.

I remember him saying there were two ways he'd do it: he'd take a trip to Alaska in winter and sit in the arctic air and freeze to death. Or he'd self-immolate. He admired the monks who did it.

I always hated it when he talked that way. I told him it was total bullshit, egotistical, exactly the opposite of the likes of Mohamed Bouazizi or Thich Quang Duc or Alice Herz or Rigzin Phuntsog or Jeon Tae-il or David Buckel. . . . He said I was right and that he therefore had come up with a practical solution. He wanted to burn himself in protest but not draw any attention to it.

God.

So what he said he'd do is if he ever saw a burning building . . .

I didn't know that. He never—

. . . was he'd run into it.

Shit, I thought he was trying to do something heroic.

That's why I wanted to have lunch. To tell you.

He told me the same thing.

He never told me. I didn't know.

It must have been impulsive or he must have thought it was fate. To come across a fire like that.

No way. That's impossible.

Of course it isn't.

And then one of us says or I say, Do the dead ever visit you in your dreams?

Sometimes. Every once in a while.

Not often enough.

I'll be at my childhood dinner table with my dead parents. I'll be the age I am now and they'll be not quite young but not yet old.

Sometimes I'll be giggling with my friend at a back table of a bar that no longer exists. Or we'll be driving through Queens in a red Civic that got totaled in 1998.

How does it make you feel? Do you like it?

It feels very normal, within the dream. Normal but nice. I don't quite notice it but afterward I remember it felt warm and close. Casual and comfortable. When I wake up, I'm grateful that I saw them, very thankful to have met them and to have been with them again. But I'm also heartbroken, a moment of passing but surging grief, as I suddenly remember that they're gone and I can't talk to them again.

The real ghosts. Our memories and our dreams.

Yeah.

I'll tell you about a story I heard, speaking about dreams and ghosts. As you know I'm interested in psychedelic drugs.

One look at you and that's obvious.

Oh come on.

Shaddup and let her talk.

And some of these plants, some of these particular chemicals, these medicinal molecules—these entheogens—have been used for centuries if not millennia by shamanic cultures—cultures that are now endangered and that have been driven to near extinction by a diseased and troubled society that is most in need of their treatment modality. Shamanic cultures, for example, like the Shipibo-Conibo in Peru, the Huichol of the Sierra Madre mountains, the Yaqui in the Sonora Desert, and the Babongo of Central Africa—

Before you go on, can I ask you a question?

Yes.

You're a middle-aged parent.

Yes. In fact, this is a parenting story.

You take your kids to piano lessons and work full-time as a nurse and do a little painting in your free time.

The paintings that are of unrecognized genius.

Let's not get carried away.

My point is you're a grown person with responsibilities. Why take recreational drugs?

I don't see them that way. Though to deny a joy-for-joy's sake kind of joyousness from these chemicals would not be wholly sincere.

My point is—

But as you know, I had some troubles with addiction when I was younger, so I wouldn't want, for example, my children to do this until they were fully grown. Yet I've found that the channel these substances have opened has actually made me more present to my children and the ones I love. And they've allowed me to get closer to my goals than I thought would be possible. Furthermore I'm in my Dante time. This is the era of Tarkovsky's *Mirror*. The *selva oscura* hour and the white day of *Зеркало*. That is: middle age. And so one's given task seems not only that of self-examination, so as to shed the neurotic and flimsy and exhausting narratives that have gone into defending one's position in the world, but also to seek some sense of serenity over the things one cannot change. And, in an important addition, the quest is also for serenity about the things that are impossible to even *know*. "The wisdom to know the difference." Though I'd heard it a thousand times, I never understood the Serenity Prayer. Not really. How can one be serene at the discovery of hopelessness and ignorance. Only through grace.

Okay, gotcha. Go on.

A particular Amazonian tribe has a training regimen for its health professionals. In order to prescribe any medicine, the young apprentice sequesters herself away and lives for a period of time, say, a month, where her entire diet centers around the ingestion of a particular plant so that the apprentice can understand and become intimate with its effects. . . . Imagine if your psychiatrist had such a studied experience with ssris. Modern mental health would be a totally different ball game! . . . And so at this point any mapping of shamanic tradition to modern medical education truly breaks down because the plant is not considered merely an isolated pharmaceutical but instead a sentient entity, or at least a being of some type of consciousness (if not a consciousness wholly comprehensible or even recognized by us), and so the young trainee isolates herself on retreat to commune and *learn from* this particular plant medicine—a medicine which isn't ayahuasca or psilocybin mushrooms or *Tabernanthe iboga* or datura or from *Bufo alvarius* or any of those that might be better known but in fact another, perhaps more esoteric one, or one now lost as the destruction of old-growth rainforest continues.

And in order to anchor her experience with this plant, she is instructed to ground her inquiry with an important, single question of her own choosing.

This young trainee chooses a question many young adults might choose, a question in fact asked by seekers of all ages and kinds. Her primary, anchoring, guiding question is this: *What is love?*

Of course she has all manner of potential answers in mind about what a romantic partnership might involve, or what sorts of sacrifices or enthrallment or tendernesses or generosity or patience or reciprocity could be included in whatever definition of love might arise. But instead of an exemplar of artisanal-vanilla matrimonial bliss or sophisticated-yet-utopian polyamorousness or noncorporate and ever-subversive queer pride, what she keeps experiencing during her nightly congress with a plant to whom she's asked the very definition of love is a sleep theater decorated in nightmare.

Night after night she is shown an architectural cutaway of a terrifying and sinister mansion in which every room holds a monstrous tableau of human viciousness: mass murder, psychic and physical torture, all varieties of sexual assault, hate crimes, geniuses of homicide and rape, profound psychopaths and sadists.

The woman bolts upright each dawn in a seismic wake of terror and agony and sadness. *What is going on?* she asks herself (and the plant). *I'm interested in peace and partnership and symbiosis! Why am I being shown all the ways humans are hateful and cruel?* But the nightmares continue every night until the last of her retreat. On that night, all the perpetrators of the horrible crimes she's witnessed suddenly appear in a ghostly crowd around her. In her dream, she looks at the legion and also at each individual simultaneously.

And then every one of these assailants—rapists and killers each—she sees spool backward in time to those often unremembered moments when it was *their* turn to be brutalized or abandoned or physically or psychically tortured. She sees the history of love's absence in their lives.

And then the dream spools them forward again into the hollow-eyed battalion standing at momentary attention in front of her—before they fade finally away. The apprentice opens her eyes and understands. The plant has given her an indirect proof in order to define love. *Love is what is missing when hate appears.*

If the conclusion had been given to her in a greeting card or a politician's slogan she would have thought too little of it even to scoff. If she'd actually given enough of a shit to attempt rebuttal, she would have hissed that *Some are born evil.* And she would have spoken of mutations, of the existence of evil, of seeds falling far far from the tree, of no room for forgiveness. But to her unthought opposition, the plant whispers about networks of lives and of causes and effects hidden in the present and recessed in ages and ages past. She remembers the question: *What did your original face look like before your parents were born?*

In a life-changing moment—epiphany is for her now more than just a word—the plant allows her to experience a wisdom enough that it permeates her essence.

So, quietly weeping, she falls to her knees, palms up. She makes obeisance to the plant. And then to the ten directions. Profoundly grateful.

AFTER AN EXTENDED BREATH, one of us responds: Yes, I understand. It's a beautiful idea. Not sure I *agree*, but it's beautiful, if maybe a bit simple.

Totally, another says almost simultaneous with the first. I know *exactly* what she means. *Exactly.* I've often thought very similarly. People are so odd, really, what goes through their minds. For example, I was once at a poetry reading.

A what?

A poetry reading.

What's that? I thought you said—

It's where people gather together and one person, or a series of people, read to the gathered.

They read what?

Poetry.

And the people listen?

Yes.

What kind of people are these that are listening?

Mostly poets.

Ah.

The audience is, yes, usually, entirely made up of : poets.

Oh, now I see.

You two stop fucking about.

Okay.

Where were we.

At the poetry reading.

Yes. Okay. Yeah.

This wasn't at a bar but at an art space, like a gallery that had been repurposed for the evening. It's important it wasn't a bar because the vibe wasn't conducive to sloppiness, to excess.

Instead the scene was relatively rarefied and formal. There was a desire to seem casual, for a costume of nonchalance and spontaneity to pervade the atmosphere—and yet this belied a very old if simple, rigid set of rules and ethics about how the evening was to proceed—

Can I ask you something?

Sure.

Was it a room full of white poets?

Primarily.

Were you the only Asian in the room?

Probably. I think so. Yes.

And?

There was another black queer poet and me and—. Wait. There was a quarter Chinese guy I know.

This is the usual, right?

For this circumstance, yes.

For this circumstance.

Yes.

Don't you get tired of it?

I'm used to it.

Have you ever tried to—I don't know. Have you tried finding other rooms? Have you tried, like, you know, to *decolonize* your own mind.

Come on.

I want to know.

You're recording this? I'm self-conscious.

Just say it. Say what's on your mind.

I have tried. I have been to other rooms, nonwhite rooms. I've thought incessantly about it. I've thought about it. I've thought and thought about it. And then I stopped thinking about it. I shouldn't stop. It's a privilege to stop. But I've stopped. I haven't really stopped but I've stopped. Mainly because I can't quote decolonize my own mental habits without disappearing, which is a step I'd be willing to take, my own disappearance, if I was capable of doing it. But I don't think I am. Yet.

But you've tried.

I haven't stopped. Even if I've said I stopped, I haven't stopped. But that white poetry room—or more exactly said: the room of art servicing the hegemony—is still one on occasion I can't help but find myself in. And furthermore I don't wish to be ashamed of it, will simultaneously campaign for a diverse and more representative future, but I am not entirely sure if the one pure option, that of opting out, is preferable to the messier and more compromised choices of, variously, staying in.

Maybe you're just weak. Or selfish.

I'm selfish?

Or weak.

Weak *and* selfish?

It's possible.

It's, yes. It's possible. Yes, maybe.

Okay, okay, so you were at a poetry reading.

I was at a poetry reading.

You were at a white poetry reading.

I was at a white poetry reading.

And?

Something unusual happened.

What happened?

It's weird to describe, difficult. Actually, it's very easy to describe but perhaps weird to feel how outside the social order it was.

What happened?

A guy in the front row pissed himself.

What do you mean?

A guy I think fell asleep and, without meaning to, urinated on himself while sitting in a chair in the front row of the poetry reading. He may've been sick or he may've been drunk, I dunno. But for whatever reason, he had an incontinent moment.

And?

Well, this is the curious thing. The room reacted with disgust and contempt. We were alerted by quick movements and the sudden scrape of chairs exploding from that rude zero point. The poet stopped reading immediately. And the poor guy came to with a start. He got up and sort of sheepishly, but maybe more in a daze, went into the bathroom to clean himself up. There was a churning murmur of disgust through the audience.

Wait, I've a side comment.

You wanna, like, let me finish my story?

Not yet.

Okay.

You ever listen to the *TigerBelly* podcast?

What's that?

It's with Bobby Lee.

Who's that?

A comedian.

He's Korean?

Yeah.

Oh, I know who you're talking about.

Oh yeah, me too. He's the worst. I hate him.

I like him.

Who is he? I haven't heard—

He's funny!

He's self-hating.

Oh, come on. He's in Hollywood.

He's dumb but brave. A kind of shock comic but goofy.

He's not dumb. He's got, like, a post-Kaufman thing going on.

Please.

He's a survivor. He's surviving. By his wits.

The comedian's job is to *risk* living in the demilitarized zone, the one between taboo and the anodyne.

Bullshit. It's about power. And I hate that racist self-mocking shit.

Get off your altitudinous horse.

Don't shit on the groundbreakers.

They knew what they were doing.

They were doing what they had to do.

They're selling a racist caricature to a white audience.

It's not fucking Johnny Yune. It's not Gedde Watanabe.

I like Johnny Yune!

My favorite was The Hip Nip.

Who's that?

Don't get heated.

I'm not getting heated.

You're getting heated.

I wouldn't shit on another artist from another generation in a past context.

I sure as shit would.

You can criticize the roles. But those guys were just trying to get by.

I can see you about to say Hannah Gadsby. Don't say it.

Hann—

Don't!

Margaret?

Oh I loved her.

She's so corny!

Aziz?

You remember Steve Park.

Which Steve Park.

He was a stand-up. He was in *In Living Color.* He wrote a manifesto about representation *in 1997.** But what I'm talking about is *Do the Right Thing.* His character was listed as just "Korean Grocer," but after he complained, they named the character "Sonny."

Yeah.

Yeah.

Yeah, I remember.

In *Do the Right Thing,* Paul Benjamin leads a crowd who wants to burn down the Koreans' store after they've burnt down Sal's Pizzeria, but the store owner, Sonny, holds them off with a broom and tells them he's *black like them.* They laugh at him, but they understand what he's saying, and they don't burn down his store.

Riiight! I remember.

Was *Do the Right Thing* before the L.A. riots?

Dunno.

Google it.

To get back to what I was saying—

1989.

So before.

---

* https://web.archive.org/web/20070928140952/http://modelminority.com
/modules.php?name=News&file=article&sid=1

Yeah. Rodney King was '92.

What year was Latasha Harlins?

To get back to what I was talking about, Jordan Peele is on the *TigerBelly* podcast.

He was!?

Yeah, Peele and Bobby Lee are tight. I didn't know. But they were both on *MADtv* together.

Oh, yeah. Right.

And right from the jump Bobby is asking Peele about the Asian guy being with the white people.

Oh, that's good.

What's he say?

In *Get Out*?

Yeah, in *Get Out*.

They talk around it for a bit.

Yeah?

And then they end up saying, Of course the rich Asian guy is with the rich white folk.

Shit.

Yeah.

Makes sense.

Doesn't make sense to me.

Of *course* he is.

Of course he is.

It's generational. Our parents are racists.

Mine aren't.

Mine sure as hell are.

Mine were. But they're getting better.

Hell, I'm racist.

Everyone's a little bit racist.

Shut the fuck up.

Just saying.

So this guy pisses himself at the poetry reading.

Oh yeah. Let's get back to that.

White guy?

Of course it is.

Yes, the dude is white. And he pisses himself, and the thing that strikes me is everyone's reaction. Everyone acts disgusted. And the guy is an immediate pariah. And he comes out of the bathroom and kind of wanders around, dazed. And around me I hear whispers, like, *Why doesn't he just leave? Jesus.* And folks are disgusted. No one asks him if he's okay, if he needs help. And these are the poets! The abject and the florid, the elegant or the abrupt, but the artform of the humiliated. The poets. And they're disgusted by a guy pissing himself.

Byron and Baudelaire they're not.

No.

The guy finally leaves. One woman goes to clean up the puddle he's left. And that's that.

That's that?

That's that.

Cool story, bro.

DAVE SAYS, "OUR FRIEND THE DYSTHYMIC AI scientist might be approaching the whole problem incorrectly."

"It might just be an impossible problem," I say.

"Deep learning is a method of pattern recognition, but this problem isn't about such recognition. It's about creation, breakthrough, eureka." Dave adds, "If the problem is one of creating art."

"But it isn't," says Muriel. "It's about showing how these prizewinners aren't art but confirmations of already understood patterns. That's the bitter prank she wishes to play."

I say, "Besides, assembly can be art. Collage is art. One person's pattern is another's eureka. The puncture of an evolutionary breakthrough, from a different point of view, can be seen as merely a next logical step in an intricately interwoven and imbricated chain of causation."

"I'm not making a philosophical point," says Dave. "Or less of one than an engineering point. The heart of a neural network as it now stands, of so-called deep learning, which is in current ascendency as a model, is its ability to digest huge amounts of data. And neural networks are also trained to solve one particular kind of problem. But *we're* not built that way. Our intelligence is relatively general, adaptable. And when we need data, what do we do? We go to the library, we ask friends, we go on YouTube. We largely offshore our data storage and only access it as necessary. And instead, what we keep at the ready are: instincts, habits, exercises in performance."

"What's your point?"

"Churning through data as a brute method will result in brute solutions. Elegant solutions—that is: human beauty and human art—come via a different architecture, because it's a different task. The heart of art is not pattern recognition. It's not perfecting an idea or making a pre-understood structure simply decoratively *novel*. Rather, it's the whole forfeiture of a dominant structure, of a pattern; it's icon breaking, paradigm shifting. And usually this deracination, this uprooting, is through the merging or combination or conflation of hitherto disparate or incompatible ideas."

"What's your point?"

"Wait," says Muriel. "It's not pattern recognition versus paradigm shift. It's a blend. It's both and neither. And cyborgian art *is* human art."

"Oh take a pill, brainiacs."

"We're getting ahead of ourselves," I say. "Let's let the dysthymic AI scientist run her experiment. Our job is only to provide the magic seed in her corpus, the spark of reality to her data set, so her pet prank can better digest the elegant variations of the toolishly competent."

"What *is* your point?"

ONE OF THE FRIENDS THEN SAYS, There's an acceptance of the leaps of a conversation that might seem entirely nonsensical to a lower-order, say, artificial, intelligence. The randomness would be hard to follow. In the same way a good joke is almost impossible to explain—and which always loses its humor through the act of explanation.

To which another friend responds, Or a conversation is not fundamentally ordered. It's a chain of grunts and agrammatical gestures, maybe not even *mostly* statements, linked by chance or by tenuous, even mistaken, associations. And, furthermore, a chain that can link back to itself or entangle itself. In a word, it's a mess. And to try to label certain threads or bits as *noise* and others as more syntactically loaded *signals* is to draw false distinctions.

Phooie. You just can't tell shit from shinola, one of us yawps back. There's a difference between your ass and your elbow, you have to admit. There *is* baby and there *is* bathwater.

I realized something about the white art room.

We're back to that are we.

Before I really decided to try to be an artist, I didn't actually have that many white friends. When I was a kid, I mean, in school. My social life was very separate from the majority, white one. It's only after I decided I was interested in this thing called art that I started finding myself more regularly in white rooms. I chose to be there because that's where the *art* was. Not of course exclusively, but practically if not largely so. Art is something symptomatic or close to wealth and power. For example, if you wanted to be a stockbroker, those rooms too are largely white. Or, if you wanted to be a politician. Certainly there might be local financial markets or trading pools that are dominated by other ethnicities. Or there are political caucuses aligned with and comprised of the nonwhite. And, of course, there are the lone, isolated mavericks. The unicorn of the independent genius is a myth that's alive and well. But if one is speaking of the painter or poet or filmmaker or sculptor in some kind of cultural and thus social setting, then these are practices which must be at least *near* wealth, which must be at least *near* power. At least to be recognized, to be discussed, to be in quote the conversation. To have the space and time to even *contemplate* these practices requires remove from at least the bottom rungs if not the entire bottom half of scarcity.

Someone responds: But you're talking about the assimilative nature of power. People bend to power. Markers of difference are used against you—until the powerful find it useful to bring you into their fold. See the construction of capital *w* Whiteness with respect to Irish and Italian immigrants. Or see the corporate assimilation of queer identity. The club of power accepts you if your othering is less profitable than your assimilation *and* if your values have been eroded to the point where they helplessly align and become synonymous *with* power.

But the hour has come when this need not be the case. In fact it may be now or never.

It's *always* never or now.

Oh god shut up, fuckwads. I mean jesus henry chrysanthemums. What are you trying to prove? The tide is beyond our approval or disapproval. Shit happens.

There was a moment of silence as we contemplated this elegant if brutally truthful rebuttal.

Do you really think Frank is dead?
    I don't know. Yeah?
    No. I mean. Yeah.
    No?

Autobiographical Interlude:

Mother

My mother is in the foreground.

I remember the only time I ever saw my mother cry. I was eating apricot pie.

—JOE BRAINARD, *I REMEMBER*

I remember my mother remembering her father.

I remember walking with my mother through the woods near her home. She points out a small purple flower. She says they called these "ring-flowers," and in her childhood they would pluck these flowers and make from their stalks a kind of ring. I remember she didn't stoop to pluck one but mimed the act.

I remember my mother remembering her family walking south on a broad road during a proxy war that had just made them refugees.

I remember one afternoon when taking a walk with her through a park, asking her something about her father, and I remember how my mother, usually reticent about the past, spooled out an afternoon of memories.

I remember telling people I usually don't remember anything before third grade.

I remember my mother remembering her family, having just become refugees, walking south on a broad road and *her* mother carrying their valuable plates on her head. My mother remembers being carried, strapped to her mother's back by a wide cloth.

I remember my mother remembering that her sisters said she would cry too loudly and how one time this endangered their lives. The family was hiding in a barley field from bombers overhead, and the family thought her cries would alert the enemy.

I remember in my childhood my mother being slightly scared of gloves because she associated them with tales she was told as a girl of North Korean agents sent to strangle children in their sleep.

I remember my mother saying there was a Korean woman she had met once, an owner of a dry-cleaning business in Columbus. She was a little older. I remember my mother remembering this other, older woman had told her she had seen her mother killed in front of her by a bomb.

Of course she was devastated, said my mother.

I remember my mother remembering that they fled to the south for perhaps a year. When they returned they discovered their home had been completely destroyed, burned to the ground.

I remember my mother remembering how a new home had been built, one they liked, but it too had to be abandoned. This time they had to sell it so they could pay the school fees for her eldest brother.

I remember my mother remembering her father as a self-taught country doctor who had schooled himself using Japanese medical books.

I remember my mother's mother knowing Japanese.

I remember my father's mother knowing Japanese.

I remember my mother remembering her father delivering babies.

That was the most regular money, she said, baby delivering.

I remember my mother, walking in the woods, and saying to me the word "forceps" and stopping to mime the pulling out of a child by the head from its womb.

I remember my mother remembering that her father treated sex workers for venereal disease, which they had picked up from, or transmitted to, American soldiers.

I remember my mother remembering a man in the village who had suffered a terrible burning of his face, and how her father—my grandfather—had cared for this man. And I remember my mother remembering this man, whom she said always called her father "father" as an honorific and as a gesture of gratitude. I remember the face of my mother remembering this.

I remember my mother walking through the woods, which she does every day, very slowly, explaining her spinal stenosis to me, and about the surgeries she's had that have made things, she says, worse. I remember my mother using the words "L4 and L5," "bulging disc," and "scar tissue."

I remember hearing once at a bar a phrase that I struggled to comprehend, which later I read was a Yiddish saying, that went: *When the father gives to the child, both laugh. And when the child gives to the father, both cry.*

I remember my mother remembering her father teaching her how to write Chinese characters.

I remember my mother remembering her father paying special attention to her education because he recognized—and declared to their family of six children—that she had a rare intelligence. Though my mother wouldn't quite put it this way.

I remember last week being annoyed that my Seamless order was late by fifteen minutes.

I remember being annoyed that the new dishwasher didn't seem to clean as well as the old one.

I remember being upset my parents didn't seem happier or more supportive of my decision to become a writer.

I remember being home and watching a K-drama with my mother in which one character, who is a wannabe filmmaker, says to his brother, "We have a saying in my business. Your own story is only interesting to you."

I remember my mother remembering how she waited under a blanket for hours and hours in her last year of high school while her brother made the daylong journey to Seoul to check on a bulletin board where the names of those who had passed the entrance exam to enter medical school would be posted.
  I remember my mother remembering how she felt when she learned she had passed.

I remember not long ago, lying in bed with my four-year-old son, his mother in the shower, waiting for him to wake up so I could make his breakfast of oatmeal, watching him breathing.

I remember my father, who is also a retired physician, saying that the entrance exam to medical school in Korea at the time also included a physical fitness portion. You had to throw a ball as far as you could. I remember my father remembering my mother throwing a ball. My mother laughs when he mentions this. She laughs and says her score on this part of the exam was *pathetic*.

I remember realizing my son's reaching the age of four has co-incided with a cloud of sadness, and I remember, as I lie in bed with him, watching him breathe, that I thought I might know why. I had a theory, but I didn't know how much faith to put in it. I remember thinking that perhaps all parents, if they're lucky, feel a sadness, an undercurrent to something good, something fortunate. But this wasn't my theory.

I remember my mother remembering her family preparing to abandon their home in 1951 to walk south as war refugees. I remember my mother remembering her mother sewing cotton balls into the lining of thin coats to add another layer against the cold.

I remember my grandmother, the woman who had sewn cotton balls into the linings of her family's coats, crying when I visited her in California, a few months before she died. I remember how I had visited infrequently.

I remember my sister and I took her out to a Mexican restaurant, and I remember my grandmother, who had carried plates on her head and my mother on her back and who had walked south with her family as a war refugee, repeatedly and reflexively (since I was the eldest male present) offering me the salsa bowl.

I remember the fact my mother came to this country in 1973 not knowing she was pregnant. I remember an odd pride when I realized this meant I was conceived in Korea.

I remember my mother remembering when they returned from the south to find their house burned down, how her father had found a carpenter to build a new house on the same land, which the family came to be very fond of. It had mud walls and a straw roof. But, to the chagrin of her oldest brother, they had to sell it to pay for his school fees, and from then on, the family lived in a series of rented rooms.

I remember my mother remembering her older brother complaining of the loss of their home.

I remember my mother saying that the older siblings had it more tough. I was too young, she said, and I didn't know we were poor.

I remember my mother remembering how, when I was two years old, she had to send me away to live with her sister-in-law's family. My aunt and her family had immigrated from Korea to Mississippi.

Decades later, I remember being a little shocked when realizing my cousins spoke English with both a Korean and an American southern accent.

I remember learning that in Korea it was a tradition to buy your parents a gift of long underwear with your first paycheck. I remember failing to send my parents any underwear.

I remember my parents having paid for all my schooling and that I've no student loans to pay back.

I remember very clearly being heartless to my mother.

I remember my mother remembering wanting to go to America quite badly, an ambition she said was one her father also had for her. He wanted her to go to medical school and then to America.

I remember my mother remembering her father learning she had gotten in to medical school. "He was *so* happy," my mother remembers.

I remember my mother remembering bringing my father to meet *her* father for the first time. In addition to telling him he shouldn't smoke, her father made my father read and translate a poem of Chinese characters.

"As a test?" I ask my mother.

"Yes, sort of," she says.

"How'd he do?"

"Good! More than 90 percent."

"Was it good enough?"

"Ha! It would never have been good enough!"

I remember my father writing my name in Chinese characters and telling me each character's meaning. I remember thinking that I cannot read my own name.

I remember being told that after nine months with my aunt in Mississippi, after I was returned to my mother, I kept calling another woman "Mommy." I remember my mother always laughed when she recalled this detail. And I remember realizing, only after having a child of my own, how much this laughter hid.

I remember my mother remembering the decision to go to America. "I was young," she said. "I had no fear!"

My mother says, "Now, I'm scared to travel on vacation!"

I don't remember much before eight. When I'm lying in bed with my son, watching him breathe, I remember that I have almost no memories prior to my eighth year.

I remember my mother remembering her father always encouraging her and her siblings to go to the United States.

But, she says, when it came time to really go, we went to their house to make our final farewell bows—and her father leaned down to her and said: *Don't go.*

When lying in bed with my son one morning, watching him breathe, waiting for my wife to come out of the shower, waiting just to wait, in the moments before I'll rise to begin making him his breakfast of oatmeal, honey, and peanut butter, I remember that I've no memory of age four—the age my son is now. I remember also that I've no memory of years five or six or seven.

I remember lying with my son and thinking about my mother and father new to this country, alone but for each other, scared but bent on survival. And I think I'm blank on that time due to witnessing their trauma, living through it—my response an erasure of memory.

And so, in my son, I see both his peaceful sleep and his childhood—but also I remember not remembering and so see just underneath or beside it something else, a negative space, my absence of memories, which points to, which *suspects*, imminent pitfalls, lurking traps, the ambient potential of tragedy—and so realize I have a throat-catching sadness that remains largely inexplicable, unremembered.

We have a saying in my business. Your own story is only interesting to you.

I remember sitting on a bench with my mother during a walk
in the woods and asking her about her father. I remember her
     remembering her father. I remember
     her remembering her father's words to her in the
     last moments before her departure to the United States
        and
during the last time she would ever see him. I remember her
remembering her father saying,

        "Don't go"—and I remember us both
           bursting out in laughter at this expected
        but unexpected punchline.

Don't go.

And Now Back to the Show

The truth is they are gone from us. The dead. Whether persisting or reformed or dispersed into oblivion, they are gone. Muriel might venture: But so are we to ourselves, from one moment to the next. But, come on, Muriel, there's a difference! And at times like this I like to quote Madonna. *Life is a mystery. Everyone must stand alone.* You know this one? . . . And now let's get back to the show. *I hear you call my name.* Back to the show. *And it feels like home.* And now back to the show. Pardon this interruption. From our sponsors. And now. Back. Back to the show. A mystery. Alone. Home. Back to the

Shaggy Dog

*One day I was an invalid. The next day I was public enemy
No. 1 being escorted to an internment camp by an FBI agent
wearing a piece.*

—NORIYUKI "PAT" MORITA

WE HAD OUR UNICYCLES IN PLACE as the freighter entered the
port city of Ras Laffan, Qatar. Carefully, Donna cracked open
the door of the shipping container in which we'd hidden ourselves for the past few weeks. I caught a teasing breath of fresh
air and glimpsed through the crack a robin's-egg sky of uninter-
rupted firmament. Somewhere nearby, according to the tracker,
the dog was on board.

As usual, Donna had come up with our plan. For months
we'd been using the tracker to get closer and closer to the dog,
but it had maddeningly managed to keep a few steps ahead of
us. It seemed to be making a steady, if wandering, route to the
Persian Gulf. In Valparaíso, Chile, we'd caught a break and
tracked the dog boarding this freighter, so, under cover of darkness, had broken into one of its stacked shipping containers. We
were fortunate in that the container was only half occupied by a
few small construction vehicles. We'd brought along an assortment of rations that turned out were only three days short.

Donna's plan seemed devious but was pretty simple. When
the freighter docked, a series of remotely controlled speakers,
which we'd managed to stash on the opposite end of the ship,
would blast Fučík's military march, "Entrance of the Gladiators."
While the crew was distracted we would slip off board. The unicycles were simply an insurance plan.

I had one foot on a pedal and another on some dunnage, sweating and tense, waiting for Donna's signal. She was watching the docking procedure through the cracked door and waiting for the right moment. While I was still suspicious of her and wondered what our endgame would be and where and when our particular ambitions would depart from each other, nonetheless I had to admit that in the past few months we were required on many an occasion to put our faith in the other and so had, almost involuntarily, grown closer. This was especially true of the past weeks when we had remained hidden together in the close quarters of the shipping container.

For example, several days ago, Donna had begun to explain her plan for getting off the ship once we docked. It included a long preface about a recent mentor. She told this to me one afternoon—not that we could tell the time of day in the darkness of the shipping container—and her face was lit by the flat white light of her phone as she tried to triangulate our location and, more importantly, confirm our final destination. As if a thought has just come to her, she looked up at me suddenly and said:

ANARCHY HAS A SHAPE, AND IT'S THE CROWD VIBRATING in the schoolyard one fine spring morning before the doors open to James Polk Junior High. I'm kind of gyrating and about to be crushed by something a girl named Agnes says. I'm pretending to be one of the cartoon characters we all know, an anthropomorphization of a pillow appropriately named: Paolo the Pillow.

What I do is I keep yelling, "I'm Paolo the Pillow!" and throwing myself at people.

Which is slightly odd as the character never does this in the cartoon, but I've simply taken Paolo's depicted and assumed-to-be soft, pliable body as inspiration so am imposing my singleton mosh pit persona on my immediate neighbors. I find this, of course, very amusing and, more importantly, an expression of a singular, superior, and hysterical sense of absurdism, not noticing at all that people are shielding themselves or walking away or putting the sharp edges of their backpacks into strategic places. I'm not even hitting people that hard, but when my Tasmanian Devil act nudges into Agnes, the self-designated but universally acknowledged queen of the eighth grade (I'm only in sixth), she pushes me, not hard, to the ground—a fall I instinctively take and dramatize for effect, landing and looking gape-mouthed with laughter in my eyes, when Agnes says, "Oh my god, you're so annoying," and then the bell rings, the doors open, and the slow pouring of preteen hormones titrates into the building while I lay on my ass a bit out of breath and brokenhearted.

The rest of the school year goes downhill from there.

I had had friends but somehow, as I've mentioned, I lost them. They began shunning me. My spastic absurdism quieted gradually, and three months later, instead of a hyperactive spark, I'd modulated first (briefly) into angry defiance and then more permanently into the affect of the unobtrusive, noiseless tween melancholic—a commonly found species of the invisible.

When I had learned that Ramona and Jerome were not my parents and that one of my mothers was Doctor Y, and when I remembered that my other mother, Maude Edith Eaton, was dead—well, it was in a peculiar but real way a great relief. For I felt that at the very least I'd found a kind of cause. *This* was why I sometimes felt crazy and aggressively nonsensical, why I behaved as if nothing mattered but the quickening pulse that came from outburst, and why such explosions of defiance or impropriety had led me to being shunned by child and adult alike. At least I'd found the source of my anger, the root cause of my sadness, and so meaning was restored to me, albeit a meaning based on affliction. I'd been abandoned. Doubly. By the two that all natural law insisted were supposed to love me unconditionally. Odd revelation.

The diabolical (or heavenly, depending on one's orientation) aspect of being human is that we are more often than not oblivious to the forces that manipulate us into our destinies. That my parents were not around must not be *their* fault, I thought to myself (in that secret language one uses to both speak to, and hide from, oneself, and with a perverse but seemingly incontrovertible logic). The fault must lie within *me*. I must not be worthy of love, or not enough so that they bothered to stick around. Of course if I'd only been *better* (in what way?), Maude wouldn't have died, and Doctor Y would not be obsessively trying to build a technology to resurrect her—or whatever she was sequestering herself halfway around the globe, away from her only daughter, in order to do.

I embarked on a series of self-improvement measures. If I could fix my flaws, if I could improve, if I could become *perfect*—so went the subconscious logic—then perhaps Maude would return from the dead or Doctor Y from her lab—and *love me again*. Of course this articulation wasn't explicit. If it was, even I would be able to recognize its fallacies, but in broad strokes *that* was the mechanism of the hidden reasoning that was pushing pushing pushing me toward impeccable conduct.

I failed.

I failed almost immediately at self-improvement. I tried to be the good girl that Ms. Patel wanted, but the required reading just sat swimming in front of my eyes for hours each night so that the requisite short answers rose only to the level of Dada sprinkled with a dash of obsequity.

What did John Brown believe?

*John Brown believed that the march for civil rights should begin
with the left foot but then the right. He believed this so much that
he gave his only begotten son to prove that all colors were equal
so he chose one for his last name that people didn't like because
it was the color of mud. He then moved to Ohio to plant fruit
trees and settled in Cleveland and started a sports franchise where
players moved in an erratic special motion to confuse their opponents and this was called science because we are all made of atoms
and eve. And speaking of colors after we watched that educational
and wonderful video in class called* Going and Growing Green
*I learned how important it is to recycle and started a habit at
our home.*

Schoolwork, no matter how hard I tried, seemed too much a
pointless effort. So I muddled through, and a constant and tremendous inner reproach resulted in only the slightest improve-
ment in my grades. In other areas though, I had more success.
Realizing that acing middle school wasn't going to happen, I
eventually turned my attention to perfecting various *skills*—
almost any skill would do, as long as I rose to become, so I told
myself, one of its more renowned adherents. This would win me
back the love I so required, or so I thought.

Which is how I ended up in clown school.

WHAT HAPPENED WAS THAT THE SCHOOL YEAR ENDED. AS
JEROME AND RAMONA weren't that interested in playing the role
of babysitter, I was free to do what I wanted. It was a hot summer, and I remember long afternoons when I would simply take
the bus into the city and then walk for hours over its radiating
pavements. I'd zigzag and turn one way or another simply to
stay in the shadows of buildings but otherwise had no goal and
no general direction, just killing time in the sizzling heat. I had

a big floppy hat with white flowers on it, and by month's end a ring of stain had discolored the daisies.

Whenever I got too overwhelmed by the heat I'd walk into a store. A bodega or a Walgreens or a 7-Eleven. And I'd stand and peer into the long rows of refrigerator doors at the assortment of drinks: all kinds of waters and iced teas in honey and lime and strawberry colors, sodas and seltzers, milk and beer. I liked pacing slowly past these glass doors and then casually stalking the store's perimeter, feeling my body cool down and become momentarily estranged from the outside heat, which, if I turned my head, I could see shimmering off the cars outside. And then I would leave, not buying anything due to some mushy mix of allowance economics and masochism—ending my anonymous tour of the store's aisles, teasing myself with the thought of a cold can. And then I'd walk like that, making rights or lefts at the whim of traffic lights, the sun, and building shadows, trying to gently remap the void, the wound of having been loved, having lost that love, and having forgotten that I'd lost it.

Once I'd recalled it, my loss was immediately familiar. The ache that I'd been feeling I could now name, which was a bitter relief. And I remember turning these thoughts over and over during those walks, plodding through the radiating city that summer, walking and walking, forgetting or trying to forget my body. Which must have been how I ended up fainting.

When I came to, I was lying on an army cot that smelled of mildew and, inexplicably, buttered popcorn. A wrinkled pudgy Asian woman was fanning me. "Oh shit, thank god," she said. "Drink this. Jesus. I was just about to call 911."

I took the glass she was offering me. "What happened?"

"You walked in here and dropped dead," she said.

"Where's here?" I said, looking around. I saw a tumble of weight lifting equipment, a deflated-looking wire that shrugged at catenary between two poles, what looked like a jumble of bowling pins, and an assortment of bow ties splayed across a makeup table.

"Whaddya think?" grunted the old woman as she rose from her kneel beside the cot. She cracked, "You're in heaven," and adjusted her pants. She stretched. "Just kidding. You're in my humble place of business: Fatty Patty's Clown College."

"Doesn't look much like a college."

"Hey, recently-unconscious one. Take it easy. This is your one-stop shop for all your clown accrediting needs. We do commedia dell'arte and Lecoq. Butoh and Bozo. Table and street magic. We do improv and movement, sword fighting and trapeze, big top and flea circus, bar and bat mitzvahs and children's parties of all kinds. Low life and high wire. We do it all."

My head ached. I sipped her ice water and tried to focus on some brightly colored suspenders hanging off a rusty nail. "Where do I sign up?" I said.

The rest of that summer I took clown lessons from Patty. Every day I'd practice making balloon animals or try to refine my clown persona or draw diagrams to figure out how best to smoosh myself into a toy car.

For the latter drill, we used sandbags, for, in the whole time I knew her, I was Patty's only student.

And at first, she didn't seem to be teaching me much. Initially she just had me do odd jobs for her around the school, which doubled as her home. I washed and waxed her car and sanded her decks and painted her fences and walls. I thought she might be taking advantage of me and wanted to complain but am glad

I didn't because the act of doing these chores turned out later to be tricky prerequisites to more formal clowning skills. And furthermore I was, in theory, doing these chores in exchange for free lessons.

In the meantime, during breaks over those long months, while sipping the root beer or munching on the peanut butter and banana sandwiches she provided, I pieced together Patty's rather epic life story.

IN 1932 KYOKO "FATTY PATTY" OHNO WAS BORN TO ITINERANT FARM WORKERS, tough issei who'd immigrated from Kyushu, Japan, in the early part of the nineteenth century. When she was a baby, she reached for her favorite toy—a wooden plate that she liked to teethe on—and took a bad tumble. Baby Patty cut her back and her injury led to infection, and she probably would have died, but the manager of the farm insisted her parents take her to a doctor, where she received the devastating diagnosis of tuberculosis of the spine. She spent the better part of the next decade in bed, most of the time in a body cast at the local charity hospital, and was told she'd never walk again. But then, when she turned my age, around ten or eleven, her parents got word of new developments in spinal surgery, and after a painful series of these, she was actually able to take steps and walk. Later on, she'd credit her success as a clown to those bed-ridden years, which she claimed gave her great powers of focus and imagination.

Then came the first of the great ironies of her life. She was finally free from her medical confinement. She could walk! But it was 1943 and the government had imprisoned all the Japanese Americans in concentration camps. Patty could walk out of the hospital, but she did so with an armed federal chaperone who took her to join her family in the camps.

YOU EVER THINK, DONNA PAUSES to ask, how they rounded up every single Japanese person they could and put them in a fucking prison? Even the kids!

I nodded and said: Rarely.

Eventually Patty and her family get out of the camps. For a while the family goes back to farmwork, and this allows Patty to build her body back up—but in grinding fashion. This is where she learns what physical work really is, through the backbreaking hard labor of collecting vegetables and fruit for pennies a box. Eventually her parents save up enough to open a Chinese restaurant in Crenshaw, in L.A. They call it the Third World Liberation Diner, and in addition to traditional diner fare, the Japanese family serves cheap and fast Chinese food to a Black and Mexican and Filipino clientele. And this is where Patty begins to realize she wants to be a clown. She'd kibitz with and charm the customers. She'd make silverware levitate and wasn't above pulling coins from kids' ears. She'd make the dessert cart disappear or "accidentally" fall face-first into a pie just to make a four-top howl.

She had dreams of going to college and even managed to get in and win a scholarship. But at the last minute her parents said they needed her help at the restaurant. It was a terrible disappointment, but Patty was an obedient daughter and so obliged. She stayed at home to help her parents. *It was just what you did back then*, Patty said and shrugged. She also glossed over the fact that within a year of this disappointment her dad was killed in a hit-and-run.

Her situation was getting increasingly claustrophobic, and she desperately wanted to leave and strike out on her own, but the only ways to do that at the time were to get a job or start a family. Patty preferred her independence too much for the latter, and while she had a series of boyfriends, she never did have kids. In those days there were very few means of employment for an ambitious woman, even if she had, like Patty did, a sharp and analytical mind. But here she lucked out again. This was an era prior to modern computers, and she landed a job in Pasadena doing intricate mathematical calculations to figure out trajectories for satellite launches. (Later, she learned about, and saw as her heroes, women like Mary Jackson and Katherine Johnson and Dorothy Vaughan.) But even though Patty was a natural at the job, she still longed for the odd buzz of performance, of stage and spotlight. She yearned, in other words, to be a clown.

She started moonlighting at the local nightclubs.

There were a few of these that were Japanese or Chinese owned, remnants of what had been called the Chop Suey circuit, and she did her clown act at these several nights a week. And after half a year of struggling like this, she got a big break. The headlining clown at a large theater had come down with the flu and couldn't go on. In desperation the producers reached out, and Patty landed the gig. It would be the biggest audience she'd ever performed for, and she was ecstatic.

This was 1968. Patty put on her best rainbow wig and her snappiest suspenders. She was pacing the green room minutes before going on when a waitress came in and started staring. The waitress looked slack-jawed and said, "You're the act!?"

"Yeah, what about it?"

"Honey, aren't you scared?"

"No ma'am," Patty said but then saw something in the waitress's face and asked, "why?"

"Don't you know who the audience is?"

"No."

"It's the twenty-fifth-anniversary reunion of the survivors of Pearl Harbor."

You can't make this shit up.* Patty had only minutes to figure out what to do. She came in on the band's upbeat entrance music juggling bowling pins but with her back to the audience. On cue, the band gave her a cymbal crash, and she threw all the pins high into the air and let them arc and crash to the floor upstage as she whipped around to face the audience.

As soon as they saw her, the audience came to a dead quiet, and throughout the thousand-seat theater you could hear the pins drop.

Even in the cheap seats they were soon grokking this was a nip clown. Patty takes a step further into the spotlight, hits her mark, and deadpans, "Before I begin, I just want to say I'm sorry about messing up your harbor."

The audience explodes. A big rolling laugh infects the entire theater. The tension that had collected almost to the point of choking—suddenly got its release. She'd won over the audience and started balancing a broomstick on her nose while juggling dinner plates. Patty's clown career had officially begun.

WAIT A MINUTE, I say to Donna.

What? she says.

Aren't you at all bothered that she had to do that?

Do what?

That she had to placate and self-denigrate herself? Doesn't it upset you that she had to make fun of herself to get those white folk to like her?

What! Are you high? They were the veterans of the mother-fucking Second World War. She had a job to do. She had to win over an impossible audience.

---

* https://youtu.be/2XpPbBoxBME

Yeah, but—

Jesus, just shut the fuck up, Donna says.

Okay, okay, okay, I say.

PATTY QUITS THE JOB AT THE AERONAUTICS FIRM and then goes into clowning full-time. After a few more years in the wilderness she gets a couple important breaks and earns regular spots in the big-top shows. Eventually she even stars in a very short-lived show on TV that happens to be the first major clown show on a national network with an Asian American lead. It only lasts a few episodes, and Patty admits that it was terrible—but still.

After a career of lows and not-just-a-few highs, in her mid-sixties, Patty realizes that her backflips and pratfalls aren't quite as nimble as they used to be, and she decides to hang up her oversized shoes. For a while an agent gets her a few acting roles. As if she were playing a racist bingo game, she quickly hits every stereotype under the sun: from mama-san to tiger mom, dispensable sidekick to kung fu master (though mostly it was: waitress or dead villager3) until eventually she decides to retire fully from performance to open up her own clown college and begin teaching.

DONNA THEN WENT ON TO EXPLAIN HOW WE MIGHT USE SOME OF THE SKILLS she'd learned from Patty in our escape off the boat. As Donna is talking I realize something about her in the story she's told. In addition to a master instructor in the clowning arts, what Donna really gained through Patty was a surrogate parent. And I'm sure it helped—in fact it was crucial—that Patty was Japanese American and that Donna herself was a biracial child. Donna's deceased mother was Anglo Canadian, but Doctor Y was, like Patty, Japanese American.

Would Donna even have been interested in clowning if Patty had been white? How odd, I thought, how race influences us so much. Obvious but odd. In a way it was race alone that made Donna take the first step on a path that profoundly changed her life.

And, I thought to myself, *what about me?* Wasn't my friendship with Frank foundationally based on the fact that we were both Korean American? I myself am second generation, speak no Korean, and was raised in the terrifyingly blank white American suburbs, and yet how important and gratifying was it that Frank was Korean—even if our mutual pastimes and interests seemed to involve only our work and our obsession with video games and psychedelics. The fact that we experienced the world through similarly marked bodies had rather outrageously turned out to be paramount to our friendship and indeed my very sense of self.

Frank was my spiritual brother whom I loved and mourned not in small part due to the fact that I'd been, for reasons beyond my understanding, removed from one world and raised in a white one. And, in our friendship, I'd seen some link to what I could have been, or what I was, somehow, *underneath* the whitewashed experiences of my life. Or at least that was what I must have been saying to myself in that secret language, hidden from oneself, just as Donna told herself that her parents must not love her due to some ungrasped flaw within. Yet while Donna's secret subconscious logic was a lie, was mine? It didn't make complete sense, yet why else was I chasing Frank's dogified ghost around the globe if I wasn't chasing some aspect of myself? What part of me had died with Frank? What part of me would never return?

PSST! DONNA WAS SAYING.

I had been daydreaming. What? I hissed back.

It's about to happen, she said, looking through the doors of the shipping container. Ready?

I tensed my body. Yes, I said. Should I play the music?

Yes, she said.

So I hit PLAY on the remote and we burst through the shipping container and pedaled fiercely for the docks. The crew caught on, but not in time. They made chase, but we had prepared for this and scattered banana peels in our wake, thus disabling their pursuit.

PAT MORITA
"THE HIP NIP"

Intelligent Artifice

*In moving between looking at an image of what we believe to
be a thing and looking at a surface made up [of] distinct, but
closely related, shifting hues and clearly defined, modulated areas,
we echo the formal tension between the painting's flatness and
spatiality. . . . It's as if a temblor has ever so slightly shifted a
deeply personal and private world, and nothing in it can ever be
put quite right again.*

—JOHN YAU ON MIYOKO ITO

At Inauthentic Sushi, we're finishing our meal. The gorgeous
owner himself brings us the check and the complimentary
dessert, green tea mochi in a small ovoid silver bowl, which
I recognize are repackaged from Trader Joe's. And which are
delicious.

Muriel says, Do you feel changed by Frank's death?

Dave says, The other day I stumbled upon these paintings by
Miyoko Ito.

Someone says, The problem with the dysthymic AI scientist's project is her misunderstanding of the genre.

Muriel says, Because for me, it has been a subtle but decisive
shift, occurring over months. Or, like with the death of my
mother, a continuing change that took place over years—and,
in fact, is ongoing.

Dave says, Have you seen Ito's paintings? Oh good. Yeah, I've come to really love them. They hold multiple spaces at once—like those optical illusions of the duck or rabbit or Rubin's vase or

Someone says, The idea of a novel isn't very rigid. It's all over the place. And at most you might say it's a work of the imagination labeled by the author as fiction, constructed with language, and greater than a certain length.

Muriel says, And, after a loved one has died, one has magical-thinking thoughts about the afterlife and reincarnation. Desperate dreams about reunion with the dead.

Dave says, the one where you can see an old woman or a young one depending on how you look. And also there's something

Someone says, Or you could say of the novel what someone once gave for the definition of poetry, that is: *All that is claimed as poetry at any given time.*

Muriel says, I've always been vaguely Buddhist but thought all that reincarnation stuff was bullshit. Superstition.

Dave says, well, there's something primary or an articulation of the subconscious in Ito's paintings, somewhat like the dreamscapes of de Chirico. Along with a conceptual provocation or pranksterism à la Magritte.

Someone says, And so on the one hand the form of the novel is so tremendously broad, even a sampling for the dysthymic AI scientist's machine, which might be a conservative or relatively uniform corpus, would contain such a variety of types and directions that mimicry, let alone artistry, would seem impossible. And yet

Muriel says, But then I heard some monk say that our present life is—Bam!—just this moment. And our past lives are all the moments before. And our future lives are simply the next moments to come.

Dave says, But there's something much more poetic in Ito than simply a mechanical optical illusion. And there's also something less dogmatic than de Chirico or Magritte. What I guess I'm trying to say

Someone says, on the other hand we've seen tremendous success with using machines to write within rigid genre lines. They do great with, like, detective, superhero, and romance stories.

One of us says, Get me?

Muriel says, I thought this could be a fairly logical, if radical, conception of reincarnation. And as an admonition toward the present moment, it directs one's primary concern to, anyway, that which, epistemologically, is the only era one can really be sure exists, i.e., this present moment.

Dave says, What I'm trying to say is that I love Miyoko Ito's work. There's a confidence in its light touch, an understanding and gradation of color plus an understanding of self, and a humor of form that's well

Someone says, Detective, superhero, and romance—at least in what we might call their hackiest and most derivative or conventional forms—have been replicated to blockbuster success by quote deep-learning machines and their human editors.

Muriel says, Bam! Just this moment.

Dave says, that I find, I find Ito's paintings, well, just that, they, they take one's breath away. You approach them and think *I've seen this before. I know what's going on here.* And then Bam! You realize Ito's recomprehended what *seeing* means.

Someone says, Some stories really are formulaic, it turns out. And we in fact enjoy this familiarity. The smooches in the rain, the trench coats and the kapows. The bams. And in these cases what can be thrilling is a work's tonal accuracy to a genre, or possibly its gentle subversion of it. The establishment of tone, however, unlike an outline of plot, is something still largely accomplished by the human quote editors and is far beyond the abilities of today's neural nets.

Muriel says, And when something profound happens in your life. Like a fatal diagnosis. Or a car crash. Or the death of a loved one. Or even something heard that fundamentally changes one's approach. You know the kind of event embodied in the phrase, *It changed my life.*

Dave says, Miyoko Ito was—like Richard Aoki, Pat Morita, Ruth Asawa, Kiyoshi Kuromiya, and practically every other Japanese American figure of a certain generation—placed in a U.S. concentration camp during the Second World War. Over 120,000 people.

Someone says, What is missing in the current manifestation of AI that makes it unable to create novel narrative has something to do with architecture. The recent advances in AI aren't because of new models of intelligence but largely were made possible by brute power, by engineering advances rather than a greater conceptual understanding of intelligence or, that proximal and vital and murky concept: consciousness.

One of us says, Huh?

Muriel says, Well, an encounter with death can change one's life. Frank's death, for example.

Dave says, Over 120,000 people. As an aside, how to read these numbers? Six million, more than half of European Jewry. Pol Pot's two million. A million in Rwanda. *Forty-five million* in Mao's Great Leap Forward. Dead. Do you ever think of what even one of those persons must have experienced? I can but rarely. And only after concentrated effort.

Someone says, Intelligent artifice—smart art—only comes with an architecture not based on solving a specific problem with nearly infinite iterations or a recognition of hidden patterns within a chaos of noise but rather

Muriel says, It still doesn't make sense, this death. Really *any* death seems wrong but in the way something is wrong for a spoiled child. The utter disbelief that one can't do something, that a favorite toy is broken. That something is *gone*. That someone is *dead*. The spoiled child rails and wails and asks: How can this be?

Dave says, Ito was born in California in 1918, but in order to avoid discrimination her family moved back to Japan in 1923. And one of the great ironies of her early life was that the day after they arrived in Yokohama a terrible earthquake hit and destroyed the city.

Someone says, the breakthrough to an artificial *general* intelligence—which is what would be required to write even a below-average novel—will need not only a design where *many* problems are being worked on simultaneously (and so to allow analogous or parallel situations and solutions to be identified between extremely disparate issues) but, more importantly,

Muriel says, That sense of discontinuity—a term cinema uses for an error in sequencing that results in the absurd—that comes from death arises from the noncoterminous nature of life's various impermanences.

Dave says, And then, fearing that Ito might contract tuberculosis, the family moved back to the United States in 1928.

Someone says, for an artificial general intelligence what must naturally arise is a sense of self, an ego, a *consciousness*. Because what must arise concurrently, simply to organize the massive simultaneity of problem-solving, is a prioritization and organization of these processes around an anchor, which is definitionally a sense of self. All that organizing activity must needs be coincident with sentience.

One of us says, Know what I mean?

Muriel says, A fundamental marker of existence, so say the passengers of the greater vehicle as well as actuaries of insurance both, is impermanence. Everything that comes into being goes out of being.

Dave says, There are two aspects of Miyoko Ito's work that operate almost independently though you could easily call them the same thing.

Someone says, So, to put it simply: What our friend the dysthymic AI scientist is trying to do is quite simply impossible.

Muriel says, But the heartbreaking detail is that things come into being and out of being *at different times!* We go around not in one grand Busby Berkeley synchronization but in an infinite variety of solo performances of all extremes of length and talent and fortune.

One of us says, Get me?

Dave says, The first is a conceptual duality in Ito's work where she simultaneously is two things: an abstractionist of geometric forms and

Someone *else* says, Of course it isn't. You're wrong. Of course what the dysthymic AI scientist is trying to do is possible. You yourself admitted some types of narratives are formulaic.

Muriel says, What I'm saying is. Life is a bitch and then you die.

One of us says, Dig?

Dave says, at the same time, Ito is a figurative painter of broad, dreamy landscapes. She manages this duality by making the recognizable or parseable or locatable objects or persons in her paintings hidden or slightly tucked away.

Someone else says, Perhaps the award-winning novel is a type of narrative that can be as deconstructed and reassembled as the trashiest of pulp.

Muriel says, But this fact of impermanence is hard to comprehend. Or, if you do, you do for just a moment. It's hard to keep in the mind.

Dave says, In an Ito painting the sun over the mountain horizon is but the slightest hump of washed-out lemon-yellow or someone's hair might be just a series of imbricated curves or maybe is it just parquet flooring?

Someone else says, A novel only has to be successful for a season to win an award.

Muriel says, You could ask yourself: *Do you ever consider how each of us will die and how that makes most of our selfish actions meaningless?*

Dave says, So one aspect of Ito's genius is this simultaneity of twin concepts: geometric abstraction and surreal figuration. That's Ito's braininess. But.

Someone else says, Think about all the lauded titles even from the past half-century, or even the past decade, and how forgotten many of them have become.

One of us says, What's your point?

Muriel says, And most of us just nod while simultaneously mumbling, *Rarely.*

Dave says, what makes you fall in love with Ito is not her brains but something else. Her poetry. Which you sense somewhat from her palette, which can be as desert as O'Keefe's or as earthy as Klee's or as emo as Munch.

Someone else says, One can think of writing the forgettable award-winning novel like a type of art forgery in the following sense.

Muriel says, We rarely confront fundamental truths, which we nonetheless believe in, but which we feel helpless and hopeless to address.

Dave says, And when she is great it is something unsayable, like any other artist. A balance of composition and layer and color that speaks of something cosmic, cerebral, risky, natural, and human.

Someone else says, *Within* an era, a forger's work can fool scholars and collectors and even the most well-trained and acute specialists. And yet

Muriel says, What's my point?

Dave says, Miyoko Ito. Look her up! Here's a painting I liked. I'll bring it up on my phone. It's called *Oracle*.

Someone else says, after a generation or so—just enough time for the culture to shift—an art forgery, which had previously fooled the most adept and knowledgeable, will appear as obviously incongruent and false to even the most average of critics. What has happened?

Muriel says, That I loved Frank.

Dave says, Here are some more of hers. Just image-search it. This is called *Sand Castle*. This is called *Steps*. This is called *Sea Window*. This one is *Gorodiva*. This is called *Mandarin, or the Red Empress*.

Someone else says, What unravels a forger's work is that aspects or details that were so integrated with our subjective experience in one era became in another *revealed*. Less implicit, less tacit.

Muriel says, My point is that I loved my friend Frank.

Dave says, This is *Act I by Sea*. This is *Kachina*. This is *Heart of Hearts*. This is *Measure for Measure*. This is *#54325*. This is *E for eclipsed*. This is *Pyramid*.

Someone else says, So perhaps a deep-learning machine is capable of this kind of forgery, i.e., presenting one era's clumsier visions of intelligence or art.

Muriel says, And because I loved my friend, I find I can't spin away from the fundamental aspect of mortality underlying my life.

Dave says. Just swipe right. This is *Past, present, interior*. This is called *Looking glass landscape*. This is called *Near the peak of Great Wall*. This is called *78 into 79*.

Someone else says, And an artificial intelligence only needs to do so for a breath, for the duration of a magic trick, before our cheaper understandings dissolve into more sturdy ones.

Muriel says, And because I can't spin away, because I'm forced to look—tethered in a way by my love for the dead, for the no-longer living—I am changed. My life has been changed irrevocably. As if reborn. Or, more accurately, as if I've been destroyed and reformed. Different but the same. Same but different.

One of us says, Still with me?

Dave says, Just keep swiping. *Miraculous Mandarin; Sea Changes; Reflection; Dream of a Dream; Habitat; Tabled Presence*. Miyoko Ito. Look her up when you can.

I say to someone, Do you want to know the kind of intelligence that makes art?

Muriel says: Transformation. Metempsychosis. Reincarnation.

I say to someone else who was nodding yes: I went over to my friend's studio the other day.

Muriel says, Bam!

I say, My friend is older, now in her eighties about.

I say, My older friend lives rather beautifully and simply.

I say, Like a nun.

I say, I love visiting my older friend's studio, which doubles as her apartment. Everything there is as neat and orderly as a monastery or submarine.

I say, I sometimes think of my older friend in that small apartment, which doubles as her art studio, and where she has lived for decades, nearly half a century, and I picture her sleeping, drawing, reading, cleaning, painting. A true believer, a renunciate, an arhat.

It's a light-filled chamber, all the walls and shelves of my friend's art studio, which doubles as her apartment, are bright white. And the sills and tables hold an assortment of thriving and elegant plants. I had come over under the excuse of perhaps buying a piece of artwork for my husband's birthday. It wasn't really a false reason—that's why I was there—but mostly I wanted to visit her and this seemed the easiest justification. She doesn't often take visitors.

My older friend—let's say her name is Helen—is an exquisite artist, self-taught, and, Dave, like Miyoko Ito, she should have received much greater recognition in her lifetime than she has. But I admit that part of me is glad that she isn't quote successful. A selfish part of me.

A selfish part of me thinks if she'd achieved the success she deserves, then there would be no way I could find myself encased in the warm sunlight of her studio, which doubles as her apartment. There'd be no way I'd be flipping through her wondrous artworks with Helen looking over my shoulder. No way she'd be even *interested* in hearing my opinions about her work. It's an intimate encounter. And the selfish part of me realizes Helen and I probably wouldn't even be friends if she'd had—like many of the members of her social circle—gotten signed up by the most blue-chip, toniest galleries in town. Her traveling companions of the time, if I named them, you'd recognize as some of the more renowned, and so also some of the wealthier, artists alive.

Even more selfishly on my part, I am glad because this misfortune of Helen's not being rewarded in a worldly way for her stunning artwork—art which I submit to you is as good and at times superior to many of her more famous peers—has tempered her worldly ambition so that, to be honest, she's more pleasant to be with. Has humbled and focused her and, in an odd way, purified her.

I mean that Helen is not bitter. Not so much and not really anymore. I mean she *was*.

Helen is an extremely ambitious and adventurous artist. How could she *not* be bitter? Knowing what she's accomplished and seeing others with less talent or rigor being given the world. It could have—and for a while it did—eat her up inside.

Her friend Frederick Moreno is a good example. Freddie painted these neat little geometric paintings that no one today cares two shits about. And they are little doodads really. Nothing bad but nothing special. But for a few years he was a darling because he could—and he would admit this—make rich people feel smart for collecting him. *This is the trick!* he'd say to Helen, under the guise of giving advice but really as a way to brag. *Make sure the rich can understand your work but just barely.*

Helen liked Freddie for his cynicism as much as she envied his success. When they were in their middle age, Freddie was buying homes upstate and on the coasts. He was vacationing in Asian and European capitals and wearing designer shirts that hid or somehow made noble his ever-expanding paunch. While Helen remained: poor, hungry, alert. In her third-story apartment, slurping soup and making the daily grind to eke out a living—of course Helen was bitter!

And Freddie was on one hand easier to envy and dismiss because he was basically a talented con artist. But there were others—and Helen wouldn't even name them for me because it was *still* too painful—who were as good as her. Or maybe even a little less so, but respectable. And they had cushy teaching gigs and retrospectives. While she paced her apartment, dined nightly on penne and canned chickpeas, and took naps for recreation.

Of course she was bitter!

But then she wasn't. Or not as much. Something snapped in her mid-sixties. Perhaps, like you're saying, Muriel, maybe Helen died. It was something like that. She died and was reborn. Destroyed and reformed. The same Helen but different. *Her life was changed,* and she let most of her anger and bitterness go. Not all of it. Her ears still perk up at opportunity. She's still ambitious, even now. But she's also realistic. The game is almost over for her. She's not going to win like she'd wanted to.

Now, she's pure like those who are pure because they never had a chance to be impure.

I'm now almost an Outsider Artist, she jokes.

Almost.

And her work, which was always good, in the past decade has become great. She makes it only for herself and whatever gods she believes in. You can tell. It's been stripped entirely of bullshit.

I flip through a recent series of her drawings. The sun is soft in her white, neat apartment where she has padded around for half a century. These are amazing! I tell her.

Thank you, Helen says.

And when the afternoon with Helen is over, I leave an idealist.

I'd entered a cynic. Someone for whom art was worldly exercise or perhaps a collection of experiences to own or to show off.

But I leave thinking art making must be something else, an individual's struggle, perhaps, with form, or the mindful juggling of an ever-unfolding pair of question-and-answer.

What is poetry? someone asked, and someone answered, All that is claimed as poetry at any given time.

Maybe Not a Ghost

Because after long enough you forget what you wanted, what you were going for, so that the search becomes where you live, its history your universe. Even if you bet your entire life on this MacGuffin. Especially if you did. Only when you do, in fact. The history's habit, landmarks, and tone what make you. So, dog, I'll throw the stick and you chase it. Yes Master. Okay dog.

Frank Exit Speaks from the Fire

I did experience thrills and brilliance as well as sweet contentments, say, of a comfortable home imbued with love. For that I'm grateful.

Also for commonplace profundities of sky, desert, ocean, tide, forest. Of the delicious rest after long and hard days. Of children's love and parents' pride and peers' admiration. Of the ecstatic relief after near-death. Of executing years of planning. Of the delirious rush just after successful improvisation.

But all was forever fading. So a kind of surfing or abiding became the best one could do. With the occasional short pit stop at, or odd half-decade of, despair or satisfaction.

Now to be done with all that.

Is this the minor dread before the nurse pokes you with the syringe? Or the sweet fall into dreamless sleep?

Or just the escalator out of the video game. No one knows until it's past important, if then.

Dongshan said, *When fire comes, fire kills you.* I never really understood that. Still don't. But I'm about to.

And when cold comes, cold kills you.

Here we go to the end. Last sprint. The infinite time of those seconds. Of not just mine but let's say anyone's. The spew of the final monologue to no one, to themselves, the raving or the final defense or the last confession. Before

exit ghost

The well-preserved ballet dancer of gunfight choreography— that is "The One"—after goofily blundering through staged promotion of his latest action film, pauses before responding to the glibly asked question from the talk show host (who himself has known grief),

"What do you think happens when we die, Keanu Reeves?"

An important beat taken.

I know that the ones who love us will miss us.

And I admit I too took pause. For the glossy man is human after all and has known death.

O you sucker, the cynic replies.

But his as good as any summation I can think of.

What one holds on to, like embers fading to coal in one's grip hours after the fire raged, are those scenes of somehow complete happiness.

Always with another. In moment of quotidian repose or casual amble. Frenzied fucking but more usually quiet cuddling. Gathered on the sofa. Whispered in bed. At lunch. Before boarding. At homecoming.

Moments of safety, satiety, connection.

But what if I'd hated more delightedly? That is, if instead of those sweet memories what was cherished were instead opportunities taken for murder and sadism, for the use of one's power over another to shame them, to *break* them. There is knowledge of war beneath that of comfort that makes the latter both more precious and more contemptible.

Beyond Good and Evil is a fantastic title perhaps for a different book.

I've always thought I could let go. If I just chose to.

Holding off of narrative time. Just speaking in the moment of burning. Of thought proceeding to thought.

No winning or losing or learning or forgetting or redeeming.

God. No redeeming.

The third Chan patriarch : *The Way is easy. Simply put down ideas of good and bad.*

>   Well, maybe next life.

Finding god in the foxhole.

(Mathangi Arulpragasam on YOLO: again and again and again and again.)

(M.I.A. dated a billionaire.)

The collected detritus in a mind about to go up in smoke.

(El Bloombito, the billionaire, drinks his beer with ice.)

I'd always, correction, *suspected* I could let go. If I chose to.

But more true: one cannot choose to. *That* isn't about suicide. That is about ego dissolution on command.

This is about suicide.

Anyway, those are just concepts now.

Or, they will be, only, in a few seconds.

This wasn't how I thought it would end.

No, I expected more shaggy dog story, an ever scheherazade-ing with an ellipsis at the end.

To be continued. Or

more clouds of conversations over lunch gatherings. Friends meeting forever.

David Byrne on heaven: There is a party. Everyone is there. Everyone will leave at exactly the same time.

My parents died a few years ago. Releasing me. Giving me permission.

They tried so hard. Strivers. Their whole lives.

Grinding their whole lives.

Bootstrap narratives.

Pop songs. Slang. Temporary language. Gossip. Moribund language. Falsetto. Fake news. Hard bop. Word

Association. Dogen: Though we love them, flowers

                    fall; and though we hate them, weeds grow.

Memories of my father, drunk, unexpectedly revealing his noble character. How he hid his grace!

Memories of my mother struggling to be affectionate for she was consummate grinder. And was allergic to self-pity.

My hatred for my archnemesis, Ms. Mistleto. The intimacy of that hate.

Fuck wisdom. Hail fury.

I was always too introspective for real fury. Which often endangered my life. The metaphoric and real adrenaline of hate, its temporary strength. But colder calculation saved my life more often.

Hail fury?

Well, the admiration maintained even now for fury, despite my denial of it, of its eluding me.

One gets overwhelmed by the number of one's enemies.

How many disastrously stupid people there are!? And how powerful the smart and evil?!

The indifferent sowing of pain for one's selfish petty desires. So many homegrown terrorists, one realizes they are the nation's birthright.

Whatever.

Centuries of pox and burnt skies and acid water—and I'm still holding out sympathy?

What-

ever.

My private burning, why? Because protest useless, hope gone. I hate you because I *loved* you.

The horror of a mother or a father killing their children before their own suicide. Imagine that insanity; imagine that conviction.

Hail fury.

The private burning because I reject the hope remaining in the public spectacle.

Powerlessness leads one to lose hope entirely—but no loss of conviction.

Fuck

Wisdom. Hail

Fury.

Don't imagine I'm not aware of your condescending notion that this is mere mistake. A weakness. A collapse. An exhaustion. Fuck wisdom.

And hail fury.

It's an acknowledgment, a recognition, a final response to despair. The fire is a home. Return.

Hail

Fury. Fuck

Wisdom.

Nearly done.

The summer week at the mountain lake. The lunches at the museum cafeteria. All those jokes at the elegant bar.

The whole fusion of good marital fucking. The glorious pathos of breakups. Angry drunk fucking. Fights where someone cries, or both of you do, in series. All the good drugs. The anonymous animal fucking. Playing video games. Live combat.

Watching TV. Listening to Grant Green stoned. All the bad drugs. All the despairing lonely fucking. The summer month at the ocean—fighting constantly.

The dinners in town. All those confessions at the bar. That friend and this friend and this friend and that friend and that friend and that one. But no longer that one or those ones. Nearly

Done. Hail

Fury. Fuck

Wisdom.

The comedian sketches a scene. The end of our world not an explosion or a millennia-long gradual attrition to zero but five to ten seconds of collective confusion, surprise, gasping for breath, collapse, and then blackout for all.

Exit ghost. End scene. Curtain.

Almost done.

Hail—

Fade out cut swipe dissolve. To black.

There was a mediocre diner near here with a cranky older wait-ress who never smiled. I ate bachelor breakfasts there often. My french fries were limp. I could have happily gone there forever but it closed.

Hail nothing.

Fuck everything.

Near done. They had split-pea soup and open-faced tuna melts. My regular order was scrambled with wheat toast, dry.

Terrible coffee.

What ghost exits?

[SAD KEANU]

Shaggy Dog

It's a Barnum and Bailey world
Just as phony as it can be
But it wouldn't be make-believe
If you believed in me.

—YIP HARBURG AND BILLY ROSE

DONNA AND I WERE PARKED ACROSS THE STREET FROM THE PLAZA HOTEL IN WENDOVER, A TOWN ON THE UTAH-NEVADA BORDER. I had the engine running and Donna was in the back peering through binoculars. It was the beginning of what no doubt would be a scorcher of a July day.

After a near miss in her bunker hidden in a suburb of Doha, and then another bit of bad luck in the walk-in fridge of a fashionable Cairo restaurant, Doctor Y and her robot dog were now back in the States. "Might be our last chance," Donna muttered under her binoculars.

In the months we'd been trying our best to catch up with the dog, Doctor Y had not been idle. Sensing that we and several government as well as corporate interests had gotten wind of her inventions' potential, Doctor Y was about to make her escape in typical spectacular fashion. She had terraformed the far side of the moon and built a small fortress, where she was planning to rocket away from the pestering calls of heads of state and immediate family.

"That's utterly impossible," I'd said to Donna when she had told me.

"Of course it isn't," Donna had said.

And so now I was behind the wheel of a recently purchased 2006 Subaru Impreza WRX STI, rebuilt from scratch, which

I had picked up on Craigslist from a bankrupt gearhead who was quick to confess he was recovering from a bad Oxy addiction. This previous owner, now a "motivated seller," said it broke his heart to part with the machine. I nodded my head in fake sympathy as I rolled up my window and then purred away indecently. The druggy mechanic had also installed a nitrous system that I was eager to test out.

"There they go!" Donna said suddenly and pointed to some shadows bobbing in the front seat of what turned out to be a Bentley Continental Flying Spur pulling out of the hotel garage.

I began following at a discreet distance.

The other driver didn't seem to spot us until the edge of town, at which point, off a full stop and when I was wedged between two suvs and a city bus, the Bentley squealed out through a red.

"Fucking go!" Donna yelled. I jumped the curb, doing sad damage to someone's nice flowering loropetalum—and got around the bus. The Bentley was way ahead, but I knew where it was going: a rocket launch site about forty miles away. I was worried though, because I knew if we got out onto open roadway, they could outrun us. I was more gutsy though, or so I thought, and dove through the parking lot of a grocery store trying to cut a corner, angering a few citizens. Someone lobbed a cabbage at the trunk.

I spotted the Bentley weaving its way through traffic about half a mile ahead. To catch up I had to sideswipe a Smart car, which pinged off the Subaru into a ditch. Seconds later we were racing out of town on a straightaway—with the Bentley pulling away.

Donna, to my annoyance, jumped over the gearbox into the passenger seat. She said, "You could ask yourself what we're really chasing." Putting on her seat belt, she continued, "Am I chasing

my mother or some illusionary and impossible plug to a hole
in my psyche, a hole that indicates I will never feel complete or
know an unconditional love? Or you," she added, "are you chasing the ghost of your dead friend or some final comprehension
of your identity and thus also chasing the 'solution' to the code of
your racially marked body?"

"Could do," I agreed, fighting against the Subaru's momentum and cutting off an oversized pickup truck with no business
in the passing lane. "But asking that I don't think would get you
very far," I added, shifting finally into sixth.

Moments later I was going 120 and accelerating, but the Bentley
was still pulling away. Each slight curve felt sickeningly lethal.
"She's losing us!" Donna shouted. "Go faster!" she screeched,
articulating an obvious demand.

Then the Bentley jumped off the road and made a straight
beeline across the salt flats. I overshot and had to do a hard fish-
tail to redirect, pitching hard and pulling the emergency brake,
spraying a crystal wave—but then was out too on the flats. I had
the gas floored and hit the nitrous. For a few seconds it seemed
we were going to catch them.

But the Bentley was a smooth criminal and started pulling
away again after I'd exhausted my juice. It was doing 180, maybe
more.

I banged on the steering wheel and Donna just stared straight
ahead. "Just don't let it get too far away," she mumbled. We were
about ten minutes from the launch site, and I wasn't sure if the
engine or our fuel would hold out, but I kept pushing the car
into the red.

After a moment, with the gas pedal still floored, I said, "For
a while I enjoyed reading what are called locked-room mysteries. Do you know what they are? Chesterton, John Dickson
Carr, Ellery Queen, Boileau-Narcejac. . . . No? A sub-genre
of the impossible-crime story where something entirely and

utterly impossible nonetheless happens. A murder that takes place in a closed room where no one could have entered or left, but in which only a corpse is found. And even later I was reading Gina Apostol's *Insurrecto* where there's the line, 'A room no one enters, a final solitude,' and which made me ask if not only Frank's death, but maybe all suicides—maybe all deaths, really—are locked-room mysteries. These are impossible cases, and all our intense sleuthing can't seem to give the corpse a narrative that makes sense. The underlying and constant mystery is the transformations between the quick and the dead."

Donna yelped and pointed. Someone—I don't think it was Doctor Y—was now leaning out of the Bentley with a gun. They were shooting at us! I did some fancy swerving.

There was a bang and the Subaru lurched.

We skidded briefly and then flipped. For a long second we were tossed around, and then, before I could react, the side airbag took me out with a solid right hook. Our front wheels had been shot out.

WHEN I CAME TO, DONNA WAS CUTTING me out of my seat. "Did you get a look at the shooter?" she asked when she saw I was conscious.

"Um, was it, I think, could it have been? Yeah. It was the dog."

"Damn," the eleven-year-old said. "Mom's moved on to the next stage."

"What's that?" I muttered.

"They've weaponized it," the kid said.

Donna cut me free. We just sat there for a few seconds. The flats were profoundly quiet. Within minutes Doctor Y would reach her secret launching pad. And shortly thereafter she would take off and sequester herself and the robot dog at her base on the far side of the moon. How would we catch up with them then? If they left this world, how would I be able to confront my dead friend or Donna her absent mother?

Donna was out of the car and starting to walk over the salt flats.

I got out and discovered I was limping, but I went after her. "Hey!" I yelled. "Where are you going?"

"To the launch site. We can follow their tracks." And it was true that the Bentley's tires left a straight line through the salt. We both started to run, though my gait was broken and a recurring sharp pain came with every other footfall.

"We'll never make it," I puffed, but Donna didn't say anything. I couldn't keep up the pace, and she too was easily winded, so we then simply fell into a sprint-walk-sprint-walk pattern that was ridiculous to observe, but what other choice did we have?

While progressing in this way, I said to Donna, "Frank was wrong when he said my grief wasn't about the death of my dog. He was implying that I'd somehow transferred my pent-up grief about the death of my father to the dog, but this isn't entirely true. It was partly true, yes. In fact, I was grieving both beings, but somehow I only allowed myself to feel the pain of my dog, only allowed myself to understand I was mourning Jofi, which I was. But while I had entered that mourning chamber using the idea of Jofi, in that space I had discovered both griefs. In the moment I entered that place, both griefs merged into one, and I wasn't able to separate the two so felt both, mourned both, not only simultaneously but in a way that the object of my grief became occluded or shifted or glimmered momentarily as in a desert mirage." I caught Donna's eye and gestured around me at the winking crystals of salt surrounding us. She just shook her head and started off again at a sprint. I limped after her.

The next time I caught up to her she said, "I don't give a fuck about your stupid dog," and I pretended not to hear her. However it did hurt my feelings.

Then Donna said, "This morning I went to my notebook and wrote, 'Much of life is drift. Most of it. And as narrative animals—especially ones in a quest tale, that is, especially as ones involved in a disguised picaresque gesturing toward an infinite ongoingness—we must needs be oriented toward the sharp turns, the plot twists, the events which change the drift's course. And yet most of life is the drift itself, as when a rock glides over a frozen lake. And one should try to pay attention to (and enjoy to the extent one is able) this majority drift. We can try to be awake to and instantly aware when the course-changing events happen, but also immediately returning to, and moment-by-moment aware of, the drift as *it* is happening. Most of life, almost all, is drift." She stopped running and started walking to catch her breath.

I made my way toward her at a broken jog, and when I passed her I said, "Oh, please."

And when I was twenty feet or so ahead of her I slowed to a walk and yelled behind me, "You're just making shit up but think that you're not. There are no collisions, events, gliding. There is only the unyielding continuation, a flux, which just happens and keeps on happening."

"Oh, what do you know!" she exclaimed in answer and then took off at a hard sprint so that she passed me and went as far as thirty feet ahead. But then she stopped and bent over and put her hands on her knees, gulping air. I made my way, chugging, toward her. By the time I got to her, her breathing was almost caught up and together we began walking at a brisk pace, continuing to trace the trail of the Bentley.

On the horizon a growing speck caught my eye.

I realized something was coming toward us. It looked like a huge television, which is exactly what it was. Someone, presumably Doctor Y, had attached this massive flat-screen to motorized wheels and was remotely controlling it toward us. I looked at Donna, but she was only staring at the machine, and we didn't break pace. In minutes it was in front of us. We tried to walk around it, but then it started rolling backward with the screen facing us. It switched on and Doctor Y's face appeared on it.

Doctor Y said:

> When I met Maude I was a young, rather moody, and depressed college professor—one who lived alone and was cynical and angry at the world. At that time I poured my energy into pranks: hacking into hospital databases and creating massive medical bills and sending them to the loved ones of insurance executives; creating natural language processing machines that would fool critics into giving gushing reviews and high-minded prizes to novels composed of unfelt strings of symbols the machines would understand as much as I understand Chinese; ordering dozens of pizzas to my boss's house; mooning the neighbors.
>
> But all that adolescent anarchic behavior was just a distraction from a confused and lonely heart.
>
> Then, one day at an otherwise terrible faculty party, I met Maude. I met your other mother.
>
> She was a rogue theoretical physicist interested in the question of whether awareness is a fundamental aspect of matter. She believed the universe was made up of information guided by a base-level consciousness that created our universe as a shadow of its higher-dimensional reality.
>
> I'd said to Maude, What?
>
> She dumbed it down for me and said, I think all matter is alive.
>
> But that's impossible, I'd said.
>
> She shrugged.
>
> In general, Maude was a pariah of the academic world and lived off of adjuncting jobs and a handful of confidence artist grants. What

she really loved doing was surfing, and she lived far out on Long Island just so she could surf in nearby Montauk.

We fell in love, and I moved in to her small rather ramshackle beach house. Those were the happiest years of my life. I'd wake up early, but Maude would get up even earlier, be out the door in predawn light to check out the waves.

I'd work for several hours while she surfed. And then I'd pack a simple lunch and take it out to her, and we'd eat sandwiches on the beach, often alone, and peer out at the infinite sea. We would talk about our future and we'd be content and laughing and grateful.

In a couple of years we had you.

I mail-ordered a kit and snagged some genetic material from one of Maude's funnier cousins. That was the easy part, but the morning sickness almost did me in. Maude nursed me through it all and took great care of both of us after the birth. You were an absolute pleasure right from the start, and we both fell utterly in love with you.

(Donna is crying—but her tears evaporate into fury. "Then why did you leave me?" she yells.)

You must believe me. We loved you and were so happy. But then Maude killed herself. I don't know why. I don't think I'll ever know. In the dark of night sometimes she'd say a thing or two about her childhood, but frankly I never understood or thought to ask more. I thought that was all in the past and that we were happy. I thought our happiness would protect us, would save us.

I was wrong.

You were still very young, and I didn't know what to do. I was lost. In my grief an idea came to me, an impossible idea. That's impossible, I said to myself. But just a moment later I would think, But of course it's not.

I dusted off my old projects. I had thought that one in particular— the AI that I had wanted to write novels—could be adapted to do

*something extraordinary. I had the idea that it could allow a kind
of communication with the dead.*

*Years went by. Pursuit of the idea led to profitable side paths,
but the primary goal kept alluding me. More years passed, and the
rewards got slimmer and slimmer to the point I almost went under.
But then one day I got it. Or, rather, I should say, my machine got
it. It spit out a novel—not really a novel but a cracked-mirror version of one. I started adapting it and integrating it into increasingly sophisticated robots. The novel barely hung together. It was
an ever frustrated and constantly interrupted episodic adventure
loosely based on my life but which had embedded in it hidden hyp-
notic suggestions and carefully dosed incepting brain viruses that
allowed the reader to—or at least made the bereft believe that they
could—talk to the dead. It was titled* Search History.

*I've been using it to talk with Maude. She's with me now. And
I'm not going to let anyone take her away again.*

AT THIS, THE MOTORIZED TELEVISION went dark and stopped
moving. I was about to knock it over in anger when a little flap
opened and something dropped onto the ground, like a turd.

The TV lurched backward and then zoomed away in the direction it had come from. I looked at Donna, who began to run.

I stopped for a second and examined what the TV robot had
dropped. It was a book. I thought to pick it up but then thought
better of it. I ran to catch up with Donna. I'd almost caught up
to her when we both stopped.

There was a rumble and seconds later we saw on the horizon
a flare and then a hot white bolt shoot skyward.

The rocket holding Doctor Y and her dog had launched.

I was about to despair but then Donna said, "We can't stop
now. Come on! I've an idea." And she grabbed my hand and we
started to run.

Acknowledgments

Joanna and Felix, I love you to the moon and back times a googolplex.

Grateful acknowledgement is made to editors at the following publications, where portions of this novel appeared in slightly different form: *Granta, The Margins, The Brooklyn Rail, 7X7,* and *Cagibi*. Special thanks to J. David Gonzalez and Breaking & Entering Press for publishing the chapbook *The Basement Food Court of Forking Paths*. Huge gratitude to the amazing and hardworking team at Coffee House Press. The definition, "All that is claimed as poetry at any given time" was first brought to my attention by Corey Frost and comes from *Poetry and Cultural Studies: A Reader,* edited by Maria Damon and Ira Livingston. Thanks to McKenzie Wark for the line "In the future we have to be as *interesting* to the AI as our pets are to us." The quote from Fran Lebowitz arguing for a technology that seems closest to human beings is from the documentary *The Booksellers* (2019), directed by D. W. Young. Thanks to Paolo Javier for tipping me off to the movie *Gook* (2017), directed by the visionary Justin Chon. GPT-3's supposed admission of a love of jokes comes from its YouTube interview with Eric Elliott, self-titled, "What It's Like To Be a Computer." Thanks to Eileen Myles for the invitation to write fiction about a dog. Thanks to Wendy Xu for the artwork on page 13. A deep bow to the seeker and cleric Shannon Steneck for the painting on page 45. Thank you to the teachers and the sangha of the Kwan Um School of Zen.

Honor and love given to Peixian Wang, Dao Li, Laura Garrity Li, and Rosanna Li.

My profound thanks also to: Donald Breckenridge, Lisa Chen and Anelise Chen of the FRC/DC, Lynn Crawford, Alan Davies, Ian Dreiblatt, Corey Frost, Jeremy Hoevenaar, Ellen Israel, Kun Boo and Keun Hee and Karen Lim, Chris Mannigan, Alex Samsky, Marya Spence, Shannon Steneck, Jamil Thomas, Cass and Danny Tunick, and John Yau.

Coffee House Press began as a small letterpress operation in 1972 and has grown into an internationally renowned nonprofit publisher of literary fiction, essay, poetry, and other work that doesn't fit neatly into genre categories.

Coffee House is both a publisher and an arts organization. Through our *Books in Action* program and publications, we've become interdisciplinary collaborators and incubators for new work and audience experiences. Our vision for the future is one where a publisher is a catalyst and connector.

LITERATURE
is not the same thing as
PUBLISHING

FUNDER ACKNOWLEDGMENTS

Coffee House Press is an internationally renowned independent book publisher and arts nonprofit based in Minneapolis, MN; through its literary publications and *Books in Action* program, Coffee House acts as a catalyst and connector—between authors and readers, ideas and resources, creativity and community, inspiration and action.

Coffee House Press books are made possible through the generous support of grants and donations from corporations, state and federal grant programs, family foundations, and the many individuals who believe in the transformational power of literature. This activity is made possible by the voters of Minnesota through a Minnesota State Arts Board Operating Support grant, thanks to the legislative appropriation from the Arts and Cultural Heritage Fund. Coffee House also receives major operating support from the Amazon Literary Partnership, Jerome Foundation, McKnight Foundation, Target Foundation, and the National Endowment for the Arts (NEA). To find out more about how NEA grants impact individuals and communities, visit www.arts.gov.

Coffee House Press receives additional support from Bookmobile; Dorsey & Whitney LLP; Fredrikson & Byron, P.A.; Kenneth Koch Literary Estate; the Matching Grant Program Fund of the Minneapolis Foundation; Mr. Pancks' Fund in memory of Graham Kimpton; the Schwab Charitable Fund; and the U.S. Bank Foundation.

THE PUBLISHER'S CIRCLE OF COFFEE HOUSE PRESS

Publisher's Circle members make significant contributions to Coffee House Press's annual giving campaign. Understanding that a strong financial base is necessary for the press to meet the challenges and opportunities that arise each year, this group plays a crucial part in the success of Coffee House's mission.

Recent Publisher's Circle members include many anonymous donors, Patricia A. Beithon, Anitra Budd, Andrew Brantingham, Dave & Kelli Cloutier, Mary Ebert & Paul Stembler, Chris Fischbach & Katie Dublinski, Jocelyn Hale & Glenn Miller, the Rehael Fund-Roger Hale/Nor Hall of the Minneapolis Foundation, Randy Hartten & Ron Lotz, Dylan Hicks & Nina Hale, William Hardacker, Kenneth & Susan Kahn, Stephen & Isabel Keating, the Kenneth Koch Literary Estate, Cinda Kornblum, Jennifer Kwon Dobbs & Stefan Liess, the Lambert Family Foundation, the Lenfestey Family Foundation, Sarah Lutman & Rob Rudolph, the Carol & Aaron Mack Charitable Fund of the Minneapolis Foundation, Gillian McCain, Malcolm S. McDermid & Katie Windle, Mary & Malcolm McDermid, Daniel N. Smith III & Maureen Millea Smith, Peter Nelson & Jennifer Swenson, Enrique & Jennifer Olivarez, Alan Polsky, Robin Preble, Jeffrey Sugerman & Sarah Schultz, Nan G. Swid, Grant Wood, and Margaret Wurtele.

For more information about the Publisher's Circle and other ways to support Coffee House Press books, authors, and activities, please visit www.coffeehousepress.org/pages/donate or contact us at info@coffeehousepress.org.